Dear Romance Reader,

Welcome to a world of breathtaking passion and never-ending romance.

Welcome to *Precious Gem Romances*.

It is our pleasure to present *Precious Gem Romances*, a wonderful new line of romance books by some of America's best-loved authors. Let these thrilling historical and contemporary romances sweep you away to far-off times and places in stories that will dazzle your senses and melt your heart.

Sparkling with joy, laughter, and love, each *Precious Gem Romance* glows with all the passion and excitement you expect from the very best in romance. Offered at a great affordable price, these books are an irresistible value—and an essential addition to your romance collection. Tender love stories you will want to read again and again, *Precious Gem Romances* are books you will treasure forever.

Look for eight fabulous new *Precious Gem Romances* each month—available only at Wal★Mart.

Lynn Brown, Publisher

SPECIAL DELIVERY

Judith Hershner

Zebra Books
Kensington Publishing Corp.

http://www.zebrabooks.com

For Tina Wittich who waited impatiently for each chapter to be finished. Also Laurie, Bev, Becky, and Karen who had faith it would happen.

ZEBRA BOOKS are published by

Kensington Publishing Corp.
850 Third Avenue
New York, NY 10022

First Printing: November, 1996
10 9 8 7 6 5 4 3 2 1

Printed in the United States of America

Chapter 1

"Nice buns, Mason."

Edwina Mason darted a quick look over her shoulder, and smiled. Addison Rivers was coming up the walk toward her. Taking one last stroke on the gingerbread trim that ran down either side of the stair rail, she laid her paintbrush carefully across the top of the open paint can at her side and arched her back. With a pleased glance at the work she'd completed, she reached up, pulling off the bandanna that had protected her long auburn ponytail from paint splatters.

She wiped her hands on the bandanna, and ambled down the worn front steps, making a slow survey of Addison's wide shoulders and tapering waist. Close-fitting regulation shorts molded his own buns very nicely. Finishing her circuit, she stopped before him to inspect his bronzed runner's legs.

"Nice legs, Rivers," she returned, dropping her voice to a soft purr as she shoved the paint rag into the back pocket of her frayed cut-offs.

Addison struggled to bring his attention away from her rounded breasts beneath her snug, paint-smeared T-shirt. His glance slid to the pink tennis shoes covering Eddie's slender feet, and the frayed toe which allowed one crimson-painted toenail to peek out. His review moved upward along Eddie's slender legs to her gently rounded hips, well-defined waist and those breasts that hinted of heaven for any man lucky enough to be welcomed into her arms. His eyebrows waggled suggestively as he met her eyes.

"Yours are better," he finally drawled with a shake of his head, his tone deep and rumbling.

Eddie's laughter filled the air as she tugged him toward the porch of her old Victorian house. "Maybe. How's the summer job?" she asked, nodding at the letter carrier's bag and uniform.

"Better than teaching summer school. How can you stand being cooped up with a bunch of teen-agers who'd rather be elsewhere?" he said with a feigned shudder.

"It's not so bad," Eddie offered, steering him away from the railing she'd been painting to the center of the wide steps. "It's only for a couple of hours in the morning when it's cool. It's so early most of the kids aren't fully awake yet."

"Ah. Subliminal teaching," he chuckled.

"Whatever works," she said easily. "Do you have time for a glass of lemonade or are you still a hard-working civil servant?"

Addison glanced at his watch. "More than enough time. I was off the clock five minutes ago," he replied, dropping his mail pouch at the foot of the stairs and sinking down to recline against the steps in the shade.

Eddie enjoyed the view of his taut muscles straining against the pale blue shirt for a moment, fantasizing about how those muscles would look without any covering at all. Blinking her eyes to push away the picture, she headed into the house.

He watched intently as she disappeared behind the screen door, his hands itching to smooth their way down her shapely derrière. He groaned, shoving his light brown, sun-streaked hair away from his face and muttered about getting a haircut when most of it fell back onto his forehead. *She's taken*, he reminded himself, turning away to stare down the tree-lined street at the kids racing bikes toward him.

"Hi, Add," the one closest to his side of the street shouted with a cheeky grin.

"Hey, Tommy. Phil," he called back and lifted his hand to wave. "And, it's Mr. Rivers to you."

The boys shot across the street, braking with a loud squeal of tires inches from the front step.

"Tell Miss Mason I'll be over tomorrow to mow her grass, will you?" Tommy said, swinging the bike around and bracing his feet for a push-off.

"Sure thing."

"Great." The boys headed back toward the street. "See you around, Add," they both shouted and laughed uproariously as Addison shook his fist good-naturedly after their retreating backs.

"Here you go, Add," Eddie called through the screen door, bumping it open with her hip. "What did Tommy and Phil want?"

Addison tilted his head back and lifted his arms over his head to take the crystal pitcher of lemonade from her hand. Bringing it to rest against his forehead, he allowed the moisture already beading the sides to cool his brow. "He'll be over to mow tomorrow."

"Okay. Want a cookie, Add?" Eddie asked, using the nickname the kids at school had given him when he'd subbed for the math teacher last fall.

She waved a plate of chocolate chip cookies beneath his nose and grinned when he closed his eyes and inhaled the aroma with relish.

"Coo-kies," he groaned, imitating the voice of Cookie Monster, his nieces' favorite television character. "Give coo-kies."

Eddie jerked the plate back with a laugh. "First the lemonade," she directed, handing him a plastic glass decorated with faded advertising for a recent movie.

"Nothing but the best for your guests, I see," Add teased, taking the glass and filling it with sparkling lemonade.

"I have to pay for the new bathtub," she said, accepting the glass from his hand and passing him the second. Lifting it to her lips, she took a mouthful and closed her eyes and let the cool liquid slip down her throat. A satisfied "ah" escaped her lips.

Addison took a hasty gulp of lemonade, trying to ease the dryness in his mouth as he watched her drink *She sure isn't making this easy,* he thought, as he struggled to conquer the impulse to draw her to him and kiss her mouth, moistened by the cool liquid. Taking a second swallow, he turned to look at the house over his shoulder.

"Damn good paint job," he said. He scrutinized the pale yellow Victorian house that shimmered in the late afternoon sun.

The house fit the quiet street, promising warmth and comfort beneath its two-story gables. He could picture bedrooms with window seats tucked into the high-peaked dormers that faced the street. Two chimneys towered over either end of the house, suggestive of romantic nights curled before a fire. Before his imagination could put a woman in his arms before that fire, he brought his attention to the wide yard beyond the steps.

Two huge maple trees, their branches tickling the sides of the house, offered shade for hot summer days and easy escape routes for adventurous children in the dark of night. A vision of a child shimmying down one of the trees teased his mind.

"Thanks for helping with it. I don't know how I'd have managed otherwise."

Eddie's soft voice drew his attention back to the present.

"What are friends for besides slave labor?" Add asked with a shrug and a wink.

They chatted with the ease of old friends for a few minutes, discussing her future plans for the stately Victorian she'd spent the last year renovating. Add reminded her of the efforts of their fellow teachers the previous weekend when she'd hosted the paint party that had turned the peeling exterior of her house from dirty gray to the sunshine yellow that now warmed its walls.

"Charles will be speechless when he sees how much I've managed to accomplish," Eddie said, brushing an auburn tendril of hair from her face. When the gentle breeze that fluttered the leaves in the maple trees blew it right back, she pushed it behind her ear.

"Yeah, Charles," Add mumbled, feeling some of the pleasure he found in Eddie's company desert him at the reminder of her invisible fiancé.

An uncomfortable silence grew between them.

"What brought you back here?" Eddie asked finally, forcing a smile to her lips and a light tone into her voice. "Didn't you deliver my mail this morning?"

"I thought I had," Addison answered as he tugged his mail bag toward him and dug deep inside. "I found this in the bottom when I was finishing the route," he explained, pulling out an envelope and holding it just beyond her reach. "You could forget old Chuck and run off with me."

"Where would we go?"

"Cleveland," he offered hopefully.

Eddie sighed. "If you'd said Columbus you could have had me. If you're only offering Cleveland, I guess I'll hang onto Charles."

"Your loss," he groaned, passing the envelope to Eddie. He nodded at the distinctive red and blue striping along the edge. "Thought this might be the one you've been waiting for."

Eddie grabbed the envelope, hugging it to her chest. A smile of pure bliss graced her lips. "It's got to be the one with Charles's arrival time. I thought it would never come. Oh, thank you," she cried, throwing her arms wide and flinging herself at Addison.

Addison's arms circled Eddie as her enthusiastic hug sent them both sprawling across the steps in a tangle of arms and legs.

"Thank you, thank you, thank you," she said as she planted kisses across both of his cheeks.

He drew in a deep breath, inhaling the scent of paint and lilacs wafting up from her auburn hair. For a moment he closed his eyes, enjoying the feel of her soft breasts against his chest.

He'd dreamed of a moment like this since the first day he'd subbed at Hendricksburg High in the math class directly across the hall from Eddie Mason's history room. The only thing stopping him from making dream into reality had been the small diamond ring on her left hand.

"Thank you," Eddie said one last time, her lips finally landing squarely on Addison's.

His arms tightened around her, drawing her closer as his lips pressed back. His tongue darted forward, tasting the contours of her mouth before slipping between her lips to sample the heat within. Eddie's fingers clutched the hair at his nape. For a moment her tongue met his, sending liquid fire coursing through his veins.

You can't do this, his brain screamed as he edged his hand down her back. *She's engaged to Charles,* his mind called when he ignored the first warning.

From the first day they'd met at Hendricksburg High School, Eddie had made it clear she was already taken and intended to be faithful during the year her fiancé was in Paris on a fellowship to the Sorbonne. Add had decided to be her friend and he'd kept his distance.

"Well, how was that?" He had gained a semblance of control over his emotions. He tried for a playful note in his voice when he repeated, "Well?"

"Extraordinary," Eddie whispered in response. She tried to focus her attention on his words and not his full lower lip, still moist from their kiss. "What? How was what?" she blurted out.

"The kiss."

Eddie opened her eyes wide. Only Charles, her fiancé, deserved a kiss like that and he'd be home any day, she reminded herself.

"Oh my," Eddie gasped. She tried to meet Addison's gaze but couldn't. Instead she focused on the half-painted railing behind his head.

"That good?" he asked when she didn't immediately respond.

"Um," she managed after licking her lips and swallowing hard. "I almost got carried away," she said at last. She felt the heat of a blush creep up her neck and into her cheeks.

"You can carry me away any time," he teased. He sat upright and moved her onto the step beside him.

Her blush deepened.

"Hey, if I can get you, the epitome of fidelity, into my amorous arms, I'm doing something right. When's Lover Boy coming home?"

Eddie's brow furrowed as she tried to remember what he was talking about. She drew in a startled breath when he reached across her, brushing against her sensitive nipples and setting off fireworks deep inside her.

"What? Oh, you mean Charles," she said, running her tongue across her lips and tasting lemonade, chocolate—and Addison.

"Yeah, Charles," Addison repeated, planting his feet on the bottom step and resting his elbows on his thighs as he looked across the street.

Eddie ripped the envelope open and quickly scanned the scrawled half-page. Her hands fisted on the sides as she lifted her eyes to the beginning of the letter and began reading again.

"He can't . . . How could he . . . Oh no!" The words exploded from Eddie to the accompaniment of shredding paper. "That weasel! That snake! That . . . toad!"

She jumped up from the steps and began pacing back and forth, waving the pieces of her letter in the air one minute and trying to hold them together to re-read them the next.

"But that's today!" she finally wailed, thrusting the paper beneath Addison's nose and then jerking it away. "Today!"

Addison watched in stunned silence.

"What's today?"

"Do you believe this?" she demanded, ignoring his question. "Do you believe the nerve of that man?"

"That toad is coming today!" she shouted at Add, scowling when he made no reply.

"So?" he asked, totally confused. "Isn't that what you wanted?"

She glowered back at him

"No!" She kicked the porch step viciously.

"Ow!" she cried when her toe connected with the step. Hopping on one foot, she clutched the injured part, teetering precariously and finally tumbling into Addison's lap.

"Hey, I'm innocent," Addison growled as her elbow connected with his ribs. "Sit still before you hurt someone."

The commanding tone of his voice penetrated the angry haze clouding her thoughts. With a sigh, Eddie stopped fighting.

"Let me get this straight," he began. He eased his arm around her shoulders and positioned her more comfortably across his lap. "Charles is coming home."

She jerked her head in agreement.

"He's coming today."

Again her only response was a nod.

"I give up," Add said, throwing his hands in the air and nearly toppling Eddie from his lap. "You're just going to have to tell me what's got you so riled."

Eddie lifted her chin proudly and tried to control the trembling of her lower lip.

"Charles is coming home today and he wants the h-house," she said softly.

"Isn't that good?"

"He wants *my* house."

Add waited patiently for her to continue.

"He's coming today to move into my house . . . with his *wife!*"

Chapter 2

"His *wife?*" Addison stared at Eddie. When she opened her mouth to explain further, he held his hand up to silence her. "Isn't that you?"

"No!" The sharp retort seemed to echo through the neighborhood.

"You mean Charles Biddington Whitney, your fiancé, holder of a Sorbonne fellowship in world economics, and all-around magnificent specimen of manhood, is returning to Hendricksburg today and bringing a wife with him?" His eyebrows rose higher and higher as he lifted a finger for each item mentioned, his eyebrows finally disappearing altogether beneath the sun-streaked brown hair that fell across his forehead.

"Yes, yes, yes," Eddie hissed, crumbling the shredded letter into a compact ball and then spreading it out again. With infinite care, she tore each piece into smaller and smaller pieces, finally tossing it into the air like confetti. "And he intends to live in *my* house."

"You, Charles, and his new wife?" Add questioned, his voice an octave higher by the last word. He grabbed the glass of lemonade at his side and took a long gulp.

"Don't be an ass," Eddie grumbled, swinging her feet against the porch step like a child, each kick intensifying as it resounded against the step back. She used the noise almost like punctuation for her next statement. "He wants me out!"

She catapulted from his lap with the last kick and began pacing the small walk in front of him.

"Tell him you don't want to move," Add suggested, relaxing and taking another sip of lemonade before reaching for a cookie.

"It's not that simple," Eddie fired back.

"Sure it is." Add grabbed another cookie and waved it in the air to make his point. "If he tries to move in, you have him arrested for trespassing. That ought to put a crimp in his style."

Eddie took a stance, fists on her hips, feet spread wide and stared at him, shaking her head.

"Why not? Trespassing and arrest. Think how that will impress his wife. Yeah, I like the idea."

"It won't work," Eddie said.

"Sure it will," Add replied, warming to the picture he'd painted. "Think lights and sirens. You could stand in the doorway screaming for help. Police leading him away in handcuffs, his . . ."

"He owns half the house."

Add's mouth dropped open in stunned surprise. "He what?"

"Owns half the house," Eddie repeated, her shoulders slumping as she dropped her gaze to her hands and the small diamond that caught the light and sparkled. With a groan, she tugged the ring from her finger and jammed it into her pocket.

When Add said nothing, Eddie hastened to explain.

"We were engaged." She paused, swallowing hard. "You know there's practically nothing to rent here in town and, economically speaking . . ."

"Charles the economist," Add threw in, disgust evident in his voice. "Let me guess. He gave you the speech about rent being pieces of paper in a box versus home ownership as equity and tax credits."

She shrugged. "We thought we'd buy an older home, fix it up while we lived in it, and sell it for a profit when he finished his doctorate."

"You thought or Charles thought?" he asked.

"Well . . . it was Charles' idea to start with," she answered, giving serious consideration to her hands again. "But I agreed. I stayed here and worked on the house while he went to Paris."

"And stuck you with all the work while he found another wife," Add finished for her with a scowl. He regretted his sharp tone the moment he saw Eddie drop her head and heard her breath catch.

"Hey, don't mind me," he said, reaching for her hand and giving it a friendly squeeze. "I only take my foot out of my mouth to change socks."

Eddie returned the squeeze and dropped to the step beside him.

Silence stretched between them for several minutes. Add finally broke it.

"So he thinks he can come back and claim your house?"

"His name is on the deed right beside mine." Eddie marshalled her thoughts as she went on. "He thinks he's doing me a favor taking on the mortgage payments. As a professor at the college, he'll make more money than I do."

"What about all the work you've put into this place?" Add indicated the newly-painted house, the colorful flower beds surrounding it and the expanse of lawn.

"He'll reimburse me." Her tone was bleak as she repeated the words from the letter before letting her head drop to his shoulder.

Add hugged her, offering what silent sympathy he could. He could feel her trembling while she struggled for control, and he waited.

He remembered the Saturdays he'd spent taking Eddie from yard sale to yard sale and hauling her purchases home in his van.

He almost laughed when he thought of their last trip and the neon purple monstrosity Eddie had transformed into a beautiful oak dining table. He'd lost twenty dollars betting her that one couldn't be stripped and salvaged.

For nine months he'd helped her make a home for another man and cursed his luck that Charles had found her first. If she'd given him one look, just one, he'd have tried to take her away from him. But she hadn't.

Eddie had been loyal to the skunk. Add doubted she knew he thought of her as more than just a fellow teacher. And look what it got her. An eviction notice and a Dear John letter all in one fell swoop. He should have fought for her, ignored the little voice that reminded him over and over that she loved somebody else.

"Want me to punch him out?" he asked, only half joking. His hand glided up and down her back, kneading the knots of tension away one by one.

"Yes. No. I don't know," she mumbled into his shoulder.

Eddie's mind filled with memories of the house. From the first moment she'd seen it, shabby and decrepit, paint peeling, steps sagging, she'd wanted it. Almost before the door was unlocked, she'd begun making plans, choosing color schemes, imagining the furniture and where she'd place each piece. Holidays, children's laughter . . . love.

Now that she thought about it, Charles had hated the house. Only the price had appealed to him. To Eddie it seemed like a dream come true.

Taking a gusty breath, Eddie finally lifted her head and focused on the house behind them. The idea of losing it hurt more than the idea of losing of Charles.

No way is Charles getting my house, she decided, straightening her spine. *He doesn't love it. To him it's just an investment for the future, his future. This was her house.* She lifted her chin proudly and put on a smile for Add.

Add noticed the smile immediately. The dull hurt that had filled her eyes was gone, replaced by the light of battle. "Good girl,'' he said, with a hug. ''How about a date since you're free Friday?''

Only quick reflexes saved him from the smack aimed for his head.

Their they laughed together for a moment, and laughter filled the air, then Add's arm tightened around her. She glanced at him and followed his intent gaze toward the street.

Parked at the curb, its doors opening, was a red Mercedes 500 SL. She gasped and stiffened when she recognized the driver climbing out.

''Charles,'' she moaned, her eyes widening. Her hand flew to her hair, pushing stray tendrils back toward the band that held its length from her face.

''*The* Charles?'' Add whispered in her ear, dodging her pony tail as she flipped it behind her back.

She could only nod.

Casting a final look at Charles assisting someone from the passenger seat, Eddie caught Add's face between her hands and swooped down to capture his lips.

For a moment Add froze as he tried to figure out what Eddie was doing. Then he threw himself wholeheartedly into the kiss, sampling her soft lips with his tongue before dipping into the wet warmth beyond.

Coherent thought fled as she teased and tantalized him, rubbing her soft breasts against his chest until he could do nothing but pull her onto his lap. Her fingers fastened in his hair, drawing him even deeper when he thought deeper was impossible.

Breathing became a necessity at almost the same moment Eddie began to draw away. He gasped for air as she nipped at his lips and planted small electrically-charged kisses along his jaw.

Charles stood, open-mouthed, midway up the walk.

Add eased Eddie away from him and drew her head to his shoulder. He allowed himself one last nip at her ear lobe.

Charles came to a stop at the foot of the steps just as Add's tongue flicked down her bare neck.

"Ahem." Charles let them know he was watching.

"Look, sweet cheeks, company," Add said, his voice raspy as his arms tightened about Eddie. "Anybody you know?"

"Mmm-hmm," she answered, lifting her head to meet his glance. She took a deep breath and leaned her forehead against his before slowly running her tongue over his lips.

"Behave yourself, woman," he growled, lifting her securely against his chest before he rose to face Charles. A squeal of outrage escaped Eddie at the sudden movement.

"Excuse me," said the slender, blond man in an outraged tone. He thrust his hand forward. "I'm Charles Whitney and you are . . . ?"

"Gonna drop her if we shake hands," Add answered, a cheeky grin on his face. Eddie nuzzled his neck. "I'm Addison Rivers. So you're Chuck Whitney. Nice suit," he added with a nod toward the silk double-breasted jacket and pleated trousers Charles wore with a white shirt and understated geometric silk-print tie. Charles seemed to be annoyed by the unsolicited nickname, as Add had hoped he would be.

"Mr. Rivers," Charles acknowledged with a nod. He focused his attention on Eddie snuggled kittenishly in Add's arms. "Edwina?"

"Charles," Eddie returned, her voice almost a purr as she ran her fingertip around Add's ear. "Were we expecting you?"

"Charles." A sultry French accent drew all eyes to the svelte blonde who rested her well-manicured hand delicately on Charles's sleeve.

"Chloe, *mon cher,* this is Edwina," Charles said, switching to French for his endearment.

Eddie felt heat wash into her face at the condemning look Chloe bestowed on her, as she made whispered comments to Charles in French. She watched the possessive way the other woman moved her hand up and down his chest, and Eddie felt her temper heat up.

"And her . . . ah . . . friend, Mr. Rivers," Charles finished, his arm circling Chloe and bringing her against his side. "This is my wife, Chloe."

"*Monsieur* Rivers," Chloe said with an appreciative gleam in her eye. She turned to Eddie and offered her hand with an almost smug smile, "*Mademoiselle Mason.*"

"Oh dear," Eddie sighed. She ran her own hand down Add's much better-developed chest and insinuated her fingers between the buttons. "This is embarrassing."

Silence descended on the four. Charles ran a finger around his shirt collar and lifted his chin as if irritated by the fit. Releasing the button of his suit he thrust his hand into his pants pocket and scrutinized the house, frowning at the paint can sitting on the porch steps.

Eddie sneaked peeks toward her former fiancé. She was satisfied that her performance had been effective only when she noted Charles' left eye narrow in the only outward expression of anger he allowed himself.

Add's arms tightened around Eddie as he searched for control of his raging hormones. He'd prayed for this for an entire school year but he knew this wasn't real.

Still, Eddie needed him to play whatever part she'd assigned him in this little farce. He couldn't let her down.

"The house is greatly improved," Charles said, his tone less than complimentary.

"Hasn't Eddie done a wonderful job?" Add bestowed a brilliant smile on the woman in his arms. "Teaching all day, scraping paint all night. She's a wonder. *Barely* left time for anything else." His eyebrows rose suggestively as he looked directly at Charles with a man-to-man grin.

"I thought we had decided on a Federal color for the exterior," Charles said, his voice low and controlled while he studiously ignored Add.

"They were so dark and dreary," Eddie said. "I wanted something sunny and bright."

"We'd decided otherwise," Charles stated coldly. "Are there other deviations to our plans?"

Eddie was furious that he would question her decisions.

"There were some problems that we hadn't anticipated and," she said firmly. "Some of the plans we made didn't seem right once I got a feel for the rooms."

If his hands hadn't been full, Add would have applauded. As it was, he was beginning to feel a strain in his shoulders from holding Eddie in his arms. He tightened them about her.

"Add, honey, why don't you put me down?" Eddie suggested, suddenly remembering where she was when she felt his muscles shift beneath her.

"Anything you say, sweet cheeks," he said, nuzzling her neck for a moment before he released her. Once he was sure her feet were on the ground, he allowed his arms to circle her waist and draw her back against his broad chest.

"Perhaps, you'll excuse us, Mr. Rivers. There are a number of things Eddie and I need to discuss," Charles said.

Eddie felt panic rise into her throat. She didn't want to be alone with Charles and his French wife. She spoke before the security of Add's strong presence could disappear.

"If you exclude my husband, don't you think we should exclude your wife?"

Chapter 3

"Your *husband?*" Charles bellowed.

Eddie prayed for a gaping hole to open and drop her through to China. *What in the world made me blurt that out?* her mind screamed, her hands clutching Add's arms tightly.

"Yeah," Add said after a slight hesitation. "After all, you know how it is." He nodded toward Chloe with a shrug and grinned wickedly.

Charles' left eye disappeared completely beneath his beetling brow while his chest puffed up like a bantam rooster with a threatened henhouse. A very pompous bantam rooster, Add decided, fighting a smirk.

Chloe's eyes narrowed, the child-like innocence slipping away for a split second to be replaced by a predatory gleam deep within. Not even the artfully created appearance of melting blue could hide their dark suspicious glitter. Her smile became condescending. "It is too bad you could not afford a ring," she said sweetly, nodding toward Eddie's hand where it lay on Add's arm.

"Ring? Oh my," Eddie managed to get out. *Tell a lie, you'll always get caught.* She prayed for inspiration. "I . . . um . . . I left it upstairs. In my bedroom."

"Sweet cheeks, you promised you wouldn't take it off again," Add said, following her lead perfectly. "She keeps taking it off to work around the house."

Eddie swallowed and tried to get something, anything, past vocal cords that were no longer taking orders from her brain. Of course, her brain wasn't helping matters any. One moment she wanted to deny the lie and laugh hysterically and the next she wanted to succumb to the tears that burnt the back of her eyes.

No, she lectured herself. *You will not give in to hysteria.* Taking a breath that sounded almost like a sigh, she forged ahead.

"I guess you didn't get my letter. This would have been so much easier if you had. How embarrassing." She sighed heavily and, she hoped, convincingly.

"I received no letter ending our engagement," Charles said, drawing himself up in offended dignity.

"Neither did I," Eddie retorted, with a telling glance toward Chloe. She wrapped her own arms about Add's as she glared at her former fiancé.

Add hugged Eddie close and dropped a kiss on her temple. "Appears the mails aren't what they used to be," he said with a wry grin. "It's a good thing we didn't send your old ring with the letter or it might have gotten lost, too," he finished, nuzzling Eddie's neck.

It was a struggle for Eddie to stay focused.

"Lost? Write?" she managed, her words soft and breathy, "Oh, yes, a long, long letter explaining . . . well, everything," she improvised, grinning impishly when Add's arms squeezed tight.

"*Chèri,*" Chloe called in husky tones, drawing their attention. "Isn't it fortunate that your little *amie* has also found someone and is not upset by our *passion épatant?*"

"Of course, *amante,*" Charles returned, finally turning his notice to her.

"Boy, am I glad that's over," Add said with a smile, blowing a gust of air from his lungs. "I thought you'd really take it hard. Eddie never wanted to hurt your feelings."

"*Certainement,* that was not my Charles's intention either," Chloe said. "When *amour* finds you, you must accept, *n'est-ce pas?*"

"Why don't you come on in the house? It's too hot outside," Add said, releasing Eddie from his embrace but claiming her hand to draw her forward.

"Yes, of course," Eddie said, beaming at him. "Why don't you come in? We really do have several things to decide." She tugged on Add's arm. "That means the check was lost. Do you think we should put a stop order on it?" she muttered loudly enough to be heard.

"Eddie makes the best lemonade," Add called over his shoulder, as he towed Eddie after him up the steps. "We were just having some to cool off. Careful of the paint can. Eddie just finished the trim before I got home."

"Add's a mailman," she said, grabbing up his pouch from the top step and trailing it after her through the screen door. "At least for the summer," she added. Add held the screen wide for Charles and Chloe to follow them into the entry hall and the living room beyond.

Charles and Chloe carefully inspected the sunshine yellow walls and pristine white woodwork that glowed in the light from the large picture window. Eddie waved them toward the white wicker furniture with its color-splashed cushions grouped before the fieldstone fireplace.

"Won't you have a seat? I'll get some fresh lemonade," Eddie said in her best gracious-hostess voice. She noticed Chloe running her hand over the table between the couch and chair before taking a seat. Her jaw clenched when she saw her inspect that same hand, as if expecting to find dirt.

Add sensed immediately what was coming. He herded Eddie across the living room, through the dining room with the oak table, and into the kitchen.

The second the door shut, Eddie whirled out of his grasp and began pacing the room.

"Can you believe the nerve of that woman? Inspecting my house as if I were her maid? And Charles. 'This isn't the color *we* chose,'" she mimicked. "There was no *we* in the choice of anything. He made a list of what he wanted and *assumed* I went along."

Jerking open the refrigerator door as she passed, she grabbed two cans of lemonade from the freezer and thumped them into the sink, turning the hot water on full force over them. Hands empty, she braced herself against the counter and dropped her head.

Leaning back against the opposite counter safely out of harm's way, Add crossed his arms over his chest and watched, waiting for the next eruption of Mount Saint Eddie. When it came, it wasn't what he'd expected.

Moisture glistened in her eyes as she whirled to face him. "His plans were terrible. He wanted to take out most of the walls on this floor to 'open up the space.' And he wanted wall-to-wall carpeting. Would you cover those beautiful hardwood floors with carpeting?" she demanded. "He wanted to get rid of all the gingerbread trim. And paint this house Boston Ivy Green or Coffee Bean Brown?"

Add allowed her to take a deep breath.

"I'm okay, now," she said, turning back to the cans in the sink.

She reached for a can of frozen lemonade, and pulled the strip around the top. Peeling away the lid, she dumped the contents into the waiting pitcher and started on the second can. "Maybe I won't add water," she mused, casting a peek at Add. "What do you think?"

"Waste of good lemonade."

"Yes, but imagine the pucker-puss Charles would end up wearing."

"I thought that was his natural look," Add said, reaching

into the cookie jar and filling a plate. "By the way, exactly why have I acquired the status of husband?"

Eddie hesitated a moment before turning to face him. She shrugged and tried to grin. "In the letter," she began.

Leaning against the counter, he asked, "You mean the one you turned into confetti or the one *you* wrote?"

"The confetti one," she explained stirring the lemonade. "One of his reasons for claiming the house as his own was that he was married." Her shoulders rose and fell in a deep sigh as she looked at Add for understanding.

"So if having a wife made him more worthy of the house, then you needed a husband to even things out," Add filled in for her.

"Exactly. And if he thought we were already living in the house . . . Well, possession is nine-tenths of the law," she finished, throwing her hands up in the air. "You won't let me down, will you?" she beseeched him, fluttering her eyelashes in a blatantly teasing imitation of some tempting heroine in a movie.

Add couldn't help but chuckle as he reached out and drew her into his arms. "Does that mean I get more kisses?"

"Maybe."

"And more hugs?"

"Probably."

"And tonight, after they leave?"

"You'll go home to your own apartment," she answered with a grin, dancing out of his arms after a kiss on his cheek.

"Spoilsport," he grumbled loudly in mock indignation. "Never want me to have any fun, just work, work, work."

"That's what slave labor is for."

Eddie passed him the plate of cookies while she collected a tray with the lemonade and company glasses. One hand on the kitchen door, she paused and gave him a wistful smile. "Thanks for helping, Add. I know I'm really asking a lot."

"I'm your friend. And your slave," he replied flippantly. He placed a kiss gently on her forehead.

Balancing the plate of cookies above his head, he rolled his shoulder against the door to the living room and swung it open, holding it for Eddie.

"Here we go," Add called to the couple who now stood near the front window whispering in rapid French as they assessed the room. "Fresh lemonade and home-made chocolate chip cookies. My favorite," he added, claiming one and taking a large bite before setting them on the low table in front of the couch and claiming one of the two chairs opposite.

"Please, have a seat," Eddie said, pouring lemonade and passing it to the pair who took seats side-by-side on the couch.

They all sat stiffly, sipping lemonade and nibbling at cookies and avoiding each other's eyes for an eternity. No one seemed willing to be the first to speak.

"What do you think about those curtains?" Add finally asked Charles. "I wasn't sure those white ruffly things were really right, but since Eddie had her heart set on them, what could I say?"

"What indeed," Charles returned, his voice low and controlled.

"Are you going to be in town long?" Eddie rushed in, trying to ease the tension with the only thing that came to mind.

"I've accepted a position at the college," Charles intoned, glowering at Add's hand where it rested just below Eddie's breast.

"I see," she replied, taking a deep sip of lemonade and searching her mind for another topic, one that might steer them away from ownership of the house until she had time to think.

"What do you think about the hardwood floors?" Add inquired. "Eddie spent hours stripping, sanding and varnishing them."

"I prefer carpet," Charles said flatly. "It makes a much quieter environment and it's what we agreed upon."

"I thought carpet was the way to go, but not Eddie. She wanted everything just perfect, no matter how much work," Add said while moving his thumb up and down Eddie's ribs, drawing closer and closer to the tender underside of her breast with each stroke.

Eddie tried hard to stifle the giggle of hysteria that rose in her throat. The situation was ludicrous. No, beyond ludicrous. She was conversing in a most genteel manner with her fiancé and that fiancé's *wife* about the way she'd decorated their, hers and Charles's that is, house while ensconced in Add's lap with his hands doing God knows what to her body while Charles droned on about what he wanted for the house.

She blinked rapidly to clear her mind and center herself in reality. Her brow furrowed in concentration as she tried to remember the last comment made.

"It did echo in here a bit before we got the furniture in and put down some throw rugs," she stammered finally. Her knuckles turned white as she clutched her lemonade glass in an effort to maintain contact with a coherent world. "It really isn't bad at all now."

Chloe leaned against Charles, whispering furiously in his ear.

Charles cleared his throat. "This is all very nice but we really do need to discuss the disposition of the house. I had explained all of this in the letter I sent."

"But *we* didn't get any letter," Add offered with a shrug.

"So you said," Charles said. "In any event, I'd like to clear this matter up as soon as possible."

"Of course," Eddie said. She leaned further into the security of Add's embrace.

"I understand how draining the expense of a home must be on your teacher's salary. Excuse me, your combined salaries," Charles nodded graciously to include Add. "Chloe and I decided that it would only be fair if we relieved you of that burden. Since I'll be teaching at the college in the fall and will be making a comfortable income it shouldn't prove a strain for us," Charles finished, a look of total assurance and benevolence turned toward Eddie.

"But . . ."

"Don't misunderstand," Charles hurried to add at a nudge from Chloe. "We're fully prepared to reimburse you for any expenditures you've made to date for minor repairs." With a nod from his wife, he extended his offer. "Of course, we won't demand you move immediately. We'll allow you time to find somewhere else to live.''

"I hope *you'll* understand why we must refuse your offer,'' Eddie spoke between clenched teeth, her fingers gripping Add's arms as if her life depended upon maintaining a secure hold.

"Surely your dear husband doesn't want to live in a place surrounded with memories of your former *amour?*'' Chloe said, her tone sympathetic but her eyes cool and calculating.

"Charles never lived here,'' Eddie fired back, shoving out of Add's embrace and rising to her feet. Charles rose as well. "Add has spent more time in this house than Charles ever did.''

"We're all kind of upset and it's getting late,'' Add began, rising and circling Eddie's shoulders to pull her against him. "Maybe we should all sleep on this and meet again tomorrow. I'll call you at your hotel to set up a time.''

"*Impossible,*'' Chloe blurted out, rising to stand beside her husband. "We are not leaving. This is our home. Charles, tell him.''

Charles patted her hand placatingly where it clutched and creased his jacket sleeve. "We intend to stay here. There's no need for other accommodations when we own this house.''

"You own!'' Eddie blurted out, hot color staining her cheeks at the slight. "You may own half of this house, Charles Biddington Whitney, but you are not staying here tonight. That's out of the question, isn't it, Add?''

He met her pleading glance and almost lost himself in the depths of her eyes.

When he remained silent, she jammed her elbow into his ribs and demanded, "Isn't it?''

For a moment Add was silent, massaging the back of his neck while he waited for inspiration. A paint smudge on Eddie's cheek and a glimpse of Chloe's expensive-looking dress gave him an idea.

"To be perfectly honest, there isn't a room for you,'' he

told them with a shrug. Dragging a handkerchief from his pocket, he swiped at the smudge of paint on Eddie's cheek.

"That won't wash," Charles said firmly. "I'm fully aware that there are four bedrooms in this house. I don't see where space should be a problem."

"Space isn't," Eddie answered sweetly, circling Add's waist with her arm. Her eyes sparkled with a gleam of pleasure at their conspiracy. "The problem is furniture."

"Furniture?" Charles demanded, his left eye narrowing suspiciously.

Turning toward Chloe, Eddie raised her shoulders as if in apology and said, "There isn't any. I just couldn't see getting furniture before I'd sanded the floors down or painted or gotten the plumbing fixed, especially after the time the bathroom drains backed up. Remember the mess?" she asked Add.

Add nuzzled her neck in order to hide a purely ornery grin. "Yeah, but I'd rather remember the clean-up and how your T-shirt . . ." he teased with a wolfish waggle of his eyebrows. He didn't even try to contain his laughter when he saw the crimson stain that crept up Eddie's neck in response to his innuendo.

"Ahem," Charles growled loudly when Eddie forced a giggle to join Add's chuckles.

When he had their full attention, Charles demanded, "Surely you're not trying to tell me you've been sleeping on the floor for the past year?"

"Of course not. There's a bed in my room," Eddie answered, her brow furrowing when Charles began to look pleased.

"Which is already quite full," Add threw in, catching sight of the same look.

"*Hospitalité* demands . . ."

"As your guests . . ."

"My guests!"

Within seconds battle was joined as they argued the merits of their side for possession of the lone bed.

Add let his mind drift, ignoring the mingled French and

English. He imagined Eddie stretched languorously across the wide bed he'd helped haul up to the master bedroom. Her skin would look like satin against the dusky rose sheets he'd helped her stretch across that same bed.

He reluctantly shook the haunting fantasy out of his head. Bad enough he should be tormented by the dream every night, now it was invading daytime hours. Besides, he was only her *husband* to balance the numbers.

"Add?" Eddie's pleading inquiry silenced the other two and drew his full attention. They all stared at him, apparently waiting for some inspired words of wisdom.

Taking a deep breath, he looked at each of the combatants, gauging the effect his suggestion might have on them. Add spoke at last. "There shouldn't be any problem sharing the house."

"Add!" Eddie squealed in horror and threw a withering glance at him.

He watched her gaze darken and could almost see flashes of lightning within them. Without her saying a single word he knew she didn't want to spend the night with Charles and Chloe under her roof, let alone in her room. Not in this lifetime.

He shrugged apologetically. "You and Charles both have an equal right to the house," he began. He had to take a deep breath to hold back the groan that threatened to escape him when Eddie's fingernails found the tender skin just above his belt line. "But I don't think Charles and Chloe would appreciate me knocking around *our* bedroom at 4 A.M. when I get ready to go to work. It seems a compromise might be in order."

Three sets of glaring eyes fastened on him.

"There are three empty bedrooms upstairs, and that futon you used when you first moved in is stashed in the attic, isn't it? They can take one of the rooms and the futon and we'll keep our room."

No one agreed outright but no one declined either.

Chapter 4

Add flopped onto his back, rumpling the coverlet that served as his mattress even more. Was it possible for a floor they'd spent hours sanding to have lumps the size of baseballs, he wondered, turning again when something gouged into his back.

With a groan of resignation he concentrated on the shifting shadows on the ceiling of Eddie's bedroom, counting the number of times one branch of the oak just beyond the window crossed another.

It wasn't easy pretending *she* wasn't in the bed two feet above him, stretched beneath the very sheets he always pictured in his dreams. He could hear every gentle, measured breath she took and it was driving him crazy. How could she sleep so peacefully when the world was topsy-turvy? How could he sleep at all when the object of every fantasy he'd had for the last year was so near and yet so far?

He closed his eyes and listened to the gentle peal of the clock that sat on the mantel above the fieldstone fireplace. He counted three tinkling bongs before it stopped.

Another hour and he could leave the room. One more hour, he assured himself, and he wouldn't have to inhale the scent of lilac talc she'd used after her shower. Wouldn't have to visualize the womanly curves tantalizingly concealed by her Minnie Mouse sleep shirt. One more hour and he could escape the prison he'd created for himself.

The only consolation for his frustrated libido was the knowledge that Charles' suffering was worse than his own. Dear Chloe had been less than pleased when Charles had reluctantly accepted the compromise Add offered. Only the thought of Add tiptoeing through their bedroom at four in the morning to find his uniform and use the bathroom had kept them out of Eddie's room and Eddie's bed.

Her invective-laced French had ricocheted about the room down the hall, impossible to miss as he and Eddie had claimed this turf. Sweet Chloe had used every one of the few French words Add had remembered from high school once she and Charles had closed their door for the night.

The tapping of a branch against the window drew his attention. He studied the branch, considering its size in relation to his own. It was a good thing Eddie hadn't gotten around to putting a hall door into the bathroom yet. If it hadn't been for Chloe needing to go through the bedroom to get there, Eddie would have had him shinnying down that tree last night so they wouldn't have to share the room. He'd have broken both legs and probably his neck, too.

"Mrs. Jackson lives two houses down," she'd hissed, once Chloe had returned to her own room. She'd shoved a pillow and the coverlet from her bed into his arms. "Neither of us will have a job next year if she tells her fellow school board members that you're sleeping at my house."

"Will it look any better if she sees me shinnying down that tree after midnight?" he'd grumbled right back.

He'd won the whispered argument in the end. As yet another muscle protested at spending the night on the floor, he questioned whether winning had been worth it.

Eddie whimpered in her sleep.

"Enough!" he grumbled, throwing the sheet off and pushing

himself, aching muscles and all, to an upright position. Grabbing the bedraggled terry cloth robe Eddie had loaned him from the foot of the bed, he tiptoed toward the door and slipped out.

Add headed for the kitchen. Maybe a cool glass of lemonade would relax him enough so he could catch a nap before heading into the post office.

Add ignored the light switch as he made his way toward the kitchen, following instead the path lit by the moon pouring in through the huge windows that circled the house.

Filling his glass from the pitcher in the refrigerator, he took the glass of lemonade to the mahogany drop-leaf table at the end of the room and sank into one of the ladderback chairs. Lifting the glass, he rolled its moist side across his forehead before taking a long sip and considering the situation.

When had things gotten out of hand? he wondered, getting up to steal some cookies from the jar on the counter. It had seemed such a simple plan. He'd pass himself off as Eddie's husband to help her save face. Of course, Charles had insisted on moving into *his* house, no matter how uncomfortable that made everyone else.

The sound of padded steps on the stairs ended his ruminations. Stepping into the shadows, he waited to see who his fellow insomniac was.

Eddie held her breath until the door clicked shut behind Add. Heaving a massive sigh, she flopped onto her back and scrubbed furiously at the tears that had been dampening her pillow since Add had turned out the lights.

Her first choice had been to scream and kick and carry on like a two-year-old, but with Add sleeping on the floor beside her, she'd decided against it. Of course, he probably wouldn't have even known. The man had dropped off to sleep the moment he'd hit the floor.

After ruling out a temper tantrum, her second choice had been equally impossible. It would have been nice to have Add hold her, safe and warm, while she blubbered out her pain and frustration. But Add had been a good friend today, and he needed his rest.

And that was another thing. What was this attraction to Addison Rivers?

It had been pure torture to lie still in the massive bed, knowing she could drop her hand over the side and touch him. Since he'd turned off the lights and lain down on the pallet beside the bed, the memory of his kisses made her heart race, stutter, and refuse to settle in her chest. Just the thought of one was enough to make her sure she'd spontaneously combust if he touched her again.

She'd tried every mental exercise she knew to focus her thoughts elsewhere. Second by second, minute by minute, she'd counted each breath she took. Inhale to a count of six. Exhale to a count of six. Inhale. Exhale. The scent of his woodsy cologne and unique male scent had filled her nostrils with each breath, invaded her being, nearly pushing her over the edge of sanity.

She had to stop thinking about him, his touch, his scent. Twitching in the bed, she sought a cool spot on the cotton sheets. The room felt stifling despite the cool breeze that lifted the sheer curtains from the bay windows facing the street. The scent of roses, honeysuckle, and lilacs from the bush beneath the window wafted into the room, mixing with Add's scent but not covering it, not erasing it from her mind.

Concentrate on finding a solution, she ordered herself. The sooner she discovered what would make Charles abandon his designs on her house, the sooner Add would go back to his own place and she could relax. She began sifting her memories of the past.

On Charles' side, he had suggested they buy a fixer-upper house, but most of the money for the down payment had been from her savings.

She felt anger building deep inside. She stretched, relaxing each muscle one by one. It didn't help.

Eddie kicked free of the twisted sheet, forcing herself from the bed and grabbing her cotton robe from the foot. Jerking the belt tight, she began pacing. Fifteen steps to the windows. Fifteen steps back to the bed. Ten steps to the bathroom door.

"I worked hard to earn the down payment," she fumed.

"I worked to make this aging relic *we* bought into a home." She turned at the bed and stomped to the bathroom door.

"I made all the mortgage payments from my salary because *he* claimed he needed every penny of his fellowship grant to live on in Paris." She headed for the window and looked out onto the empty street.

"I took care of the termites in October, the busted furnace in January, and the leaky plumbing in February. My stars and garters, have I really been such a wimp?" she demanded of herself. She headed for the door to the hall.

"The only thing *you* did," she hissed jerking open the door and speaking to an imaginary Charles, "was sign your name to the deed for my house."

Fury carried her down the stairs, through the moonlit house and to the kitchen.

Eddie flipped the light switch at the same time she pushed the kitchen door open. She couldn't stop the yelp of surprise when she bumped into a light-blind Add.

"You scared the life out of me. What are you doing here?" she demanded, careful to keep her voice low.

"Getting a snack," he explained, holding up his fistful of cookies. "I thought you were asleep."

Eddie stomped past him and pulled a glass from the cupboard before yanking the refrigerator open and reaching for the lemonade. "I had a nightmare," she said quickly.

"Bad one?"

"Wall-to-wall brown carpet, beige walls, massive furniture," she went on. "Charles sitting in the middle of everything with a calculator, toting up how much my work is worth."

Add tried not to laugh at her disgruntled description. He

failed to control one side of his mouth which insisted on lifting and twitching. Eddie spied it.

"This is not a laughing matter," she retorted, thumping her glass on the table and dropping into a chair.

He claimed the seat next to hers.

"I can still punch him out. Just give the word."

"I'll keep it in mind," she said, stealing one of the cookies from his hand.

They sat in companionable silence, drinking lemonade and munching cookies as the old school clock on the wall over the table ticked away the minutes.

"He's not getting my house," Eddie stated some time later.

"Never thought he would," Add replied, noting the firm set of her chin and her squared shoulders with satisfaction.

"I'm open for suggestions," she said, turning to face him.

Add leaned forward and landed a smacking kiss on her forehead before leaning back in his seat.

"We play it out. All you have to do is hang on my every word, drown me in adoring glances, and agree with everything I say," he directed flippantly. "Within days our saccharine sweetness and total devotion will overwhelm him, and he'll slink away into the night, schlepping his French wife with him."

Eddie considered the possibility and dismissed it. "He doesn't let go easily, especially if there's money involved. If he finds out I lied about you and me, he's likely to blackmail me into selling him the house."

"How do you figure that?" Add asked, leaning back and throwing one arm over the back of his chair.

"He'd go to the school board, claim we're living in sin and setting a bad example for the kids." She met his glance briefly. "Add, we could both lose our jobs, and I'll lose the house for sure. I can't ask you to jeopardize your job because of my problems."

Fear and uncertainty cut deep lines into her smooth brow.

She blinked rapidly, struggling against tears and tried to smile when he patted her shoulder tentatively.

"You didn't ask, I offered," he assured her, beginning to rub the knots of tension from her neck. "Besides, if he gets this house, I won't get my afternoon lemonade."

"Well, we can't let that happen."

"Look, if he can drop someone as gorgeous as you for that plastic doll upstairs, it's obvious the man's short on postage and how can he get anywhere without proper postage?"

His droll words brought a weak smile that slowly widened into a grin, exposing the half dimple that generally hid in her left cheek.

"We're in this together, until all the lemonade dries up. Deal?"

Eddie couldn't contain the laugh his silly words had been intended to draw from her. "Deal," she answered, clasping his hand and dragging him close enough to kiss his cheek.

The squeak of the kitchen door drew their attention.

Charles, scuffed his way into the room, with one hand shielding his eyes from the bright light.

"It's 3:37 a.m." he growled, looking at the watch on his arm. "Don't you have any consideration for those who might possibly be sleeping in this house?"

"Oops, sorry," Eddie said, an unrepentant twinkle in her eyes.

Add lifted his glass high in one hand. "Want some lemonade? Cool you off."

"No," Charles said rudely, his gaze fixed on Eddie's womanly curves beneath her thin robe and nightshirt.

She was disconcerted by Charles' intense scrutiny. It was a struggle not to clutch her robe more securely around her and hide her breasts beneath folded arms.

"Silly man," Eddie purred, taking Add's glass from him and setting it on the table before sliding onto his lap. She dropped her voice, making it husky with innuendo. "Let's not cool off."

Add's body responded instantly to her wiggling bottom in his lap and he wrestled for control. It was a losing battle.

"Okay," he answered, circling her with his arms and drawing her snugly against his chest, just before her lips descended on his.

Sparks flared the moment her lips touched his, driving out all thought of Charles. Eddie teased his parted lips, barely touching his tongue with fire before he joined her, trailing his tongue across her full lower lip before tasting the tart inner side.

Neither saw Charles flush scarlet. Nor did they hear the solid *thwack* of his hand against the kitchen door as he shoved his way out. They were too lost to the sensations blazing to life as their lips explored new and sensual territory.

"Oh my," Eddie gasped, coming up for air and resting her forehead against Add's.

Add groaned, and took a deep breath.

"I think he's gone," she murmured her fingers playing absently with the hair at his nape.

"Are you sure?" He let his fingers trail slowly past each indentation of her spine as he waited for her answer.

"Don't know."

The old school clock on the wall chimed four o'clock.

Add drew in a deep breath and blew it out slowly. "Maybe I should get ready for work," he told her, loath to let her leave his embrace.

"Maybe you should," she agreed reluctantly, slowly lifting her head, her hands trailing from his broad shoulders to his deeply-muscled chest.

"What time . . ."

"When will . . ."

They spoke together, then stopped, waiting.

Add inhaled and grasped her waist firmly in his hands, holding on for one more second before setting her on her own feet. He waited until he was sure she had her balance before releasing her. He noted the clearing of his senses with regret.

"I've got to jog over to my place for some fresh clothes," Add said, taking a step back.

"Do you want to borrow my car?" Eddie asked, suddenly missing the warmth of his arms.

"No, thanks, the exercise will do me good." Add backed toward the outer door.

"Add?"

"Yeah?"

"That robe. Little awkward for jogging in, isn't it?"

Add dropped his gaze to the borrowed robe and shook his head in bemusement. "Guess I'd better change first. Wouldn't want to upset Mrs. Jackson."

Eddie nodded.

"I'll change and be off," Add explained, heading for the door to the dining room. "I'll run the water in the shower for a few minutes while I'm up there."

"If you think that's best," Eddie answered, watching him from beneath her lowered eyelashes.

"Be down in a few minutes," Add said, slipping out the door.

Eddie listened to his step on the stairs, and waited for the creak of the loose board three steps into the bedroom. When she heard the sound of rushing water, she sagged into her chair at the table and dropped her head into her hands.

Good lord, what was happening to her?

Chapter 5

Eddie pulled the oven door open just as the timer went off. Taking a deep, appreciative sniff, she pulled the trays of chocolate chip cookies out and set them on the counter just as Tommy, one of her students, knocked and poked his head in the back door.

"Hey, teach. I'm here," he said, swaggering into the kitchen and taking up a position on the opposite side of the counter before reaching for one of the cookies.

Eddie smacked his knuckles with her spatula. "I just took those out of the oven. You'll burn your fingers."

"Ouch. I just wanted a snack before I got started," he complained, pulling his hand back sharply. "Us growing boys need lots of food to keep going. You wouldn't want me to faint on your lawn, would you?"

Chuckling as she set the cookie sheets next to a mixing bowl half-filled with dough, Eddie pulled open the refrigerator door. "How about a soda to keep you going while you get started?" she offered.

"Sure," he answered, easily catching the can she tossed him. "That might be enough sugar to get me through the next five minutes."

"Well, drink it then," Eddie urged him, returning to her cookie dough. "You can have some cookies when they're cool."

"Good deal," Tommy called, whistling and pushing his way out the door.

Eddie heard the lawn mower roar to life. She began whistling the tune Tommy had planted in her brain while she slid the next batch of cookies into the oven.

"What is that god-awful noise?" Charles demanded, shoving his way into the kitchen a few minutes later.

"Tommy's mowing the lawn," Eddie answered, taking another batch of cookies from the oven. "That green stuff just keeps growing."

Charles slapped his clipboard and calculator on the kitchen table and sat down. Ignoring Eddie, he began flipping papers and punching numbers into the machine.

"How much did that dining room table cost?" he asked as Eddie wiped the counters.

"Twenty dollars. Somebody had painted it a ghastly purple—" Eddie stopped talking when Charles began punching numbers again.

Eddie had the counters cleared and everything except the mixer put away in a matter of minutes. She'd just bent down to put it away in the cupboard when Charles asked, "What did you pay for that maple secretary?"

"Umh," she muttered. "I got it at a garage sale for fifty dollars," she finally answered absently, arranging the mixer in its niche in the cupboard. She didn't offer any details of its deplorable condition. The piece had been used in someone's garage to hold cans of car oil.

Charles went back to punching numbers and flipping papers. Sudden silence alerted her to the eminent arrival of Tommy. Taking a plate from the cupboard, she piled several of the cooling cookies on it and set it on the counter along with another can of soda.

"I couldn't stand it any longer." Tommy pulled open the kitchen door.

"I'm ready for you," Eddie told him, assuming a defensive stance behind the cookies.

Tommy tromped into the room, grabbing a cookie and the can of soda almost before coming to a stop.

Eddie leaned over the counter, pulling her face into a frown as she inspected the trail of new-mown grass on the kitchen floor from the door to Tommy's grass-stained sneakers. "Get the mop, kid. I'm not cleaning that up," she said, putting on a fake scowl.

"No! Not the mop!" Tommy exclaimed dramatically, clowning and stepping away from her. He bumped into Charles' elbow with the next step, sloshing lemonade over the sides of the glass in the man's hand.

"Can't you watch where you're going?" Charles growled, grabbing napkins from the holder in the center of the table.

"Hey, mister. I'm really sorry." Tommy deftly caught the towel Eddie threw him to mop up the mess.

Charles glared at him. Piling his scattered papers and calculator onto the clipboard, Charles scowled at Eddie as he pushed back his chair and marched from the room.

"Geez, teach. I didn't mean to do it." Tommy busily cleaned up the puddle of lemonade still on the table.

Eddie joined him at the table, cookie plate in one hand, her own glass of lemonade in the other. She took a towel and finished the job, lobbing the damp cloth into the sink when she was done.

"I'm sure you didn't, Tommy," as she claimed the chair Charles had vacated. "How's summer going?"

"Too fast." Tom launched into details of his most recent activities as they shared the cookies, Charles and his rude behavior soon forgotten.

* * *

Well, the house is still standing, Add thought, turning down Elizabeth Street toward Eddie's house. He pulled his ten-year-old van into the drive and parked behind Charles' sports car. Grabbing the mailbag stuffed with his clothes, he slid from the cab and checked the small box in his pocket. He headed for the back door.

"Hi, sweetie, I'm home," he called loudly, entering the kitchen and inhaling the tangy smell of home-made spaghetti. His eyes rested on an attractively disheveled Eddie at the sink.

He dropped his bag at the door and pulled her into his arms, twirling her around the floor in an impromptu dance.

"Add, they're not here. There's no need for you to be affectionate now," Eddie pointed out, her hands clutching his shoulders.

"Just keeping in practice," he pointed out, twirling her one last time. "Got to stay in character. Wouldn't want me to slip at a crucial moment, would you?"

Eddie shook her head and gave a halfhearted smile, enjoying herself more than she wanted to admit.

"Miss me?" he whispered into her hair.

"Argh," she mumbled, burrowing into his arms and burying her head in his neck.

"Bad day?" he asked, hugging her tight against him and inhaling the strange mix of garlic, lilac, and pure, unadulterated Eddie.

"The worst," she grumbled, pushing out of his arms.

"Want to tell hubby all about it?" he said, following her to the sink and resting his hands on her shoulders. He began massaging the tight muscles he found.

"How long have you got?" she returned, picking up a head of lettuce and rinsing it under the tap.

"All night. Unless you had something else in mind."

She flicked her wet fingers at him and leaned against the sink, relaxing into the strong fingers that seemed to be working magic on her neck pain.

"Those people are driving me insane," she finally said when his hands stopped rubbing and dropped to encircle her waist.

He nuzzled her neck, running his tongue toward her ear until she squealed in delighted protest. "Talk or I tickle," he threatened her, his fingers inching along her ribcage.

"The bed's too soft, the water's too cold, the stairs are too narrow, the rooms are too small, there are no closets, the bathroom's antiquated, I shouldn't have paid fourteen hundred dollars for a new furnace," she blurted out, turning to fling her arms around his neck as she gulped for breath. "Yellow is too bright a color, the trash compactor is not a necessity, I should have had the house completed by now, and my hair's too long."

Add leaned back to get a good look at Eddie. Lifting one hand he smoothed damp tendrils from her face that had escaped her French twist. One by one he pulled the pins from the twist, tangling his fingers in the hair that fell in silky waves down her slender back.

"I like your hair long," he told her, catching a handful to bury his nose in it.

"So do I. Thanks for the vote of acceptance," she said with a sigh and a kiss for his beard-roughened cheek before turning back to the vegetables waiting in the sink.

Add released her and picked up a knife, attacking the radishes that waited attention.

"Was there anything they *did* like?" he asked after decapitating several little red bulbs.

"My summer school job," she explained, ripping lettuce leaves violently.

Add chuckled. "Let me guess. They like it best because you were gone."

"And making money," she added. "Don't forget that."

Add began scraping the carrots waiting beside the sink, "Want to explain the rest?"

Eddie reached for the tomatoes.

"The futon was too soft so they bought a bedroom set with a firm king-size mattress. The delivery man slipped trying to get it upstairs and gouged the paneling. Once they got the set into the bedroom, there was hardly room left to walk.'' She made a sharp slice through the tomato in her hand for each difficulty detailed.

Fearing for her fingers, Add clasped her hand tightly in his and tried to make her smile. ''They didn't appreciate the claw foot tub, even if it does hold two comfortably,'' he said. ''Because it doesn't have a whirlpool sauna attachment. Two staid yuppies couldn't possibly appreciate sunshine yellow versus safe beige. They dislike the compactor, just on principle.''

He raised his arm, finger extended in the air, as he hurried through the rest.

''And everyone knows one woman can accomplish more than two people, especially if one is a penny-pinching economist, and their luggage arrived and *Madame* has no place to hang her clothes.''

Eddie joined his laughter.

''You wouldn't believe the luggage. Apparently Chloe was a big time model in France,'' Eddie explained. ''Even if there'd been a closet, it couldn't have held half of what she's brought.''

''So, we're entertaining the rich and famous,'' Add said in mock excitement.

''Entertaining?'' Eddie asked, her eyebrows rising. ''More like being personal maid. She actually demanded padded hangers. Do you know how much those things cost, especially when you need hundreds?''

''Well, I'm impressed,'' he replied. ''So what happened to all these wonderful clothes without a closet?''

''I strung a clothesline in the bedroom next to theirs,'' she said softly. ''Made the biggest walk-in closet I've ever seen,'' she added, slicing the tomatoes with less vigor and more finesse.

Add turned his attention to the carrots he was dicing. ''That make her happy?''

''Not really. She deplores having to leave their *chambre á coucher* to get her clothes,'' Eddie said, her voice mimicking Chloe's heavy French accent perfectly. ''I think they wanted me to say I'd tear out the wall between the two rooms to please them.''

"Poor woman," Add said, tossing the carrots into the salad bowl as Eddie finished with the tomatoes. "I'm living out of my mail pouch and she's worried about walking down the hall.''

Eddie shot him a questioning glance.

"Just a change of clothes and some grubbies," Add said, hands raised in surrender. "I'm not asking for a bed or anything. Unless you're offering to share.''

"Not on your life, Rivers," Eddie said, feeling a strange tingling in the pit of her stomach at his suggestion.

He shrugged and lifted the lid from the pot of sauce, inhaling the fragrant mix deeply before covering it. Grabbing his bag from beside the door, he asked, "Have I got time for a shower?''

"If you make it very, very short," Eddie said, taking a big pot from the cupboard and beginning to fill it with water.

"I almost forgot," Add said, coming back to her side and reaching into his pocket. "To soothe *madame*'s sense of what's right.''

Eddie took the small box he offered and stared at the soft gray velvet thing. Her eyes stung and she blinked rapidly to hold back the tears that threatened. *Silly,* she chided herself. *You weren't emotional when Charles proposed. Of course, Add hasn't proposed or anything,* she reminded herself.

She lifted tear-sparkled eyes to meet Add's.

"Well, open it.''

"But . . .''

"Look, I just thought it'd make things look right," Add explained. He took out an antique ring made of rose-colored gold set with a large oval amethyst, and claimed her left hand. "Didn't think you'd want a diamond," he explained as he turned her hand to admire the ring on her slender fingers.

"Add, it's beautiful," she returned, staring at the pale lavender stone. She was frowning when she glanced back up at him. "You shouldn't have. It must have cost a fortune.''

"Sure I should have. Doesn't every husband get his wife a ring?" he teased, releasing her hand to chuck her under the chin. "How do you know it didn't come from a Cracker Jack box?"

Eddie ran a finger tip over the simple but elegant ring. She stared at it rather than Add as she responded. "This is not from a Cracker Jack box."

"Don't believe that one, huh? My grandmother never did either, even though grandpa told her that a thousand times."

"Oh, Add, I couldn't wear your grandmother's ring. She must have meant you to give it to your own wife," Eddie said. She tugged at the ring to get it off.

"For now, you're my wife," Add insisted, sliding the ring back down her finger. "Besides, Granny would have gotten a real hoot out of this circus."

"Circus is right," Eddie said, still eyeing the ring dubiously. "What if I lose this?"

"We'll get another box of Cracker Jacks," Add answered easily, heading for the door again. "I'll just go grab that shower."

"Remember, short," she told him absently, smoothing her finger once again across the ring. "I want one before supper, too, and after the marathon soak Chloe indulged in, I doubt there's any hot water left in the whole town."

"We could make it longer if we shared," he offered, ducking through the door before the dishrag Eddie tossed could land.

"Since we're all here, let's go over some of the notes I took today," Charles said, sitting down his wine glass on Eddie's cut-work linen table cloth. The kitchen clock chimed six.

Eddie gasped, frantically checking her watch before shooting Add a beseeching glance and jumping to her feet.

"Ball game?" he asked, leaning back in his seat and trying not to laugh at the stunned expressions on Charles' and Chloe's faces.

"Six thirty," she said, surveying the dining room table and the remains of supper. She picked up the serving bowls and made a beeline for the kitchen.

"Edwina," Charles called after her, his voice sharp and his left eye narrowing.

"Sorry, Charles, not now," she called from the kitchen, the sound of running water drowning out anything else she might have said.

"Why not?" he demanded with a scowl, grabbing his wine glass before she could claim it as she made a quick circuit of the table and returned to the kitchen.

"Eddie's got a ball game in half an hour," Add explained, pushing to his feet and collecting the plates and silverware.

"Surely an evening's entertainment isn't as important as the disposition of this house," Charles stated, his left eye almost disappearing.

"It's not entertainment, it's her job," Add said as he picked up the napkins and wadded them into a ball.

"Her job? Since when has Edwina known anything about sports?"

"Eddie knows enough to have a ten and one season," Add returned, the muscle in his jaw ticking wildly while he waited for the next comment. He could almost see the calculator in Charles' brain pounding away. When Charles said nothing, he headed for the kitchen.

Eddie stood at the sink, soapsuds to her elbows as she rapidly washed and rinsed the dishes.

"Why don't you use the dishwasher?" Add asked, lifting a towel from the rack in front of the sink and beginning to dry.

"Never put good china in the dishwasher," she explained, reaching for the next plate.

"Charles' rule," Add whispered in her ear.

"Mother's rule," Eddie said, carefully laying the rinsed plate aside.

"You'll never get finished in time," he pointed out, stepping clear of the wet dishrag she swung at him.

"Don't you think I know that? But I can't leave these things just sitting around. The girls are coming over after the game and ..."

"Breakage. Say no more. Go to the game," Add directed, taking the dishrag from her hand and urging her toward the door. "I'll take care of things here."

Eddie hesitated a moment, scanning the dishes and then Add's large hands. "You're sure?"

"For every dish I break, you can have a finger," he offered, waggling all ten at her. "Just imagine a math teacher with no fingers to count on."

Eddie couldn't suppress her laughter as she bolted for the door, slinging her purse over her shoulder as she made her escape. "I'll hold you to that and I'll owe you," she called, pulling the door shut behind her.

Chapter 6

Eddie didn't try to silence the exuberant girls who tumbled out of the cars parked in front of her house. Victory over their arch-rivals, Emerson High, for the first time in six years with a score of fifteen to three didn't allow noise control to be a consideration.

However, excited or not, the mud-covered victors were not getting past her front door. "Back door," she shouted over their hoots and whistles. "Head for the back door."

She waited for the last stragglers to get ahead of her before pushing to the front of the pack and climbing the porch stairs.

"I take it you won," Add called, throwing open the door and shaking the hand of each surprised girl who passed him.

"Fifteen to three," someone cried, leading the rest in chanting the numbers loud enough for the whole neighborhood to hear.

"Congratulations, Coach," he greeted Eddie, throwing an arm around her shoulders and ushering her to the kitchen table.

Eddie gaped at the table and turned a tremulous smile to the man who'd prepared a victory celebration for her team. Orange and black streamers fluttered between the hanging lamp over the table and the walls. Bowls stood waiting beside not one, but two, ice cream freezers and every topping known to mankind. In the center of the table was a mound of hot dog buns. She sniffed the air appreciatively. The scent of hot dogs, onions, tangy mustard, ketchup, and pickle relish blended and set her stomach to growling.

"You didn't eat much supper," he whispered in her ear before dropping his arm and taking up a position in front of the kettle of boiling water and hot dogs. "Get 'em while they're hot," he bawled, passing out paper plates and dogs to the girls as they filed past.

Eddie was the last in line. Taking her plate from him, she nodded toward the dining room and lifted her eyebrows in question.

"Out," Add explained softly, nudging her toward the table and the waiting condiments before adding, "What happened to them? Change from Tigers to Mud Hens?"

"What?" Eddie asked in confusion.

"Your team. When did it rain?" he asked, motioning toward the mud-splattered girls attacking everything edible in sight.

"Don't need rain when the Fire Department decides to vent the hydrants onto the field an hour before game time," she explained, slathering her hot dog with mustard and onions.

"How thoughtful." Add began to pull cans of pop from the refrigerator and pass them to the girls who lounged around the kitchen, many taking seats on the floor.

"Not nearly as thoughtful as you. Thanks for everything," Eddie said, claiming the stool near the telephone and setting her plate on the kitchen counter. "Thanks for washing my good dishes, too."

"Don't thank me for that. They're all sitting on the dining room table," he said, leaning against the counter facing her. "I didn't know where anything went so I told them that you were very particular about how they were put away."

"Did they say anything?"

"They said they'd be back late," Add returned with a shrug.

"I wonder if asking them to this impromptu get-together was too much?"

"You what?" Eddie yelped, grinning sheepishly when the girls all stared at the two of them. "You invited them to stay ... for this?" she hissed, waving her arm to encompass her disheveled team and the fast food bonanza.

"Moved them out of here faster than the word fire," Add assured her, spearing another hot dog for one of the girls.

Eddie shook her head in bemusement and munched on her hot dog.

"Hey, Coach. Who's the blonde guy with the red Mercedes parked out front all day?"

"Did you see him? Real yuppie type but the car's not bad."

"Yeah, but did you catch the slinky on his arm?"

"Heard anything from your boy friend?"

"Saw them moving in that new bedroom set today. Can I have your old one? It is so-o cool."

Eddie said nothing, letting the rapid barrage of questions float over her. She hadn't considered these complications when she'd invited the girls over. How could she possibly explain the madness that had become her life to anyone, let alone a bunch of teen-agers?

"Hey, Mr. Add, what you doing here?"

The reasonable question stopped Eddie mid-chew. Her glance snapped to Add, her eyebrows rising alarmingly. How could she explain Add's presence, never mind Charles and the 'slinky'? Too embarrassed to meet Add's eyes, she concentrated on adding condiments to her hot dog.

Without blinking an eye, Add passed another hot dog across the counter and answered evenly, "Cooking hot dogs."

"Ah, come on. You sweet on Coach?"

Twelve pairs of curious eyes were immediately glued to Add's face. Amazed to discover heat rising in his cheeks, he eyed the girls, scratching his head and considering what possible explanation would satisfy a bunch of romantic, terminally-curious teen-age girls. Before he came up with a single possibility, they gave him a whole list.

"Nah, they're just platonic."

"What's plutonic?"

"Not plutonic, platonic. That's like really good friends but no kissing or good stuff."

The comments and speculation flew about the room as each girl offered her own explanation for Add's presence and the identity of the blonde guy with the slinky.

"I have the definitive," stated the most mud-spattered girl in the lot. Her frizzy ponytail bobbed wildly as she nodded her head in complete assurance and waited for the full attention of her cohorts. When all eyes were fixed on her and silence filled the room, she proceeded.

"Mr. Add, as Coach's friend, has come to her aid in a moment of tribulation."

Hoots from the others drowned her out for a moment. She waited patiently for silence.

"The blonde guy is the old boyfriend, the one we never ever saw. He's brought along his new girlfriend to stick it to Coach. Mr. Add is simply pretending to be Coach's new boyfriend so she won't feel dumb with the the the slinky hanging around."

Add had to consciously pull his mouth closed.

Eddie stared in dumbstruck amazement at her team.

All eyes fixed on the two, who shot questioning glances back and forth but couldn't come up with a single thing to say.

"Amazing, simply amazing," Add finally said with awe.

"Nothing to it. I read my mom's romance novels," the creative genius explained. She bowed to a rousing round of applause from her teammates.

Add's deep, rumbling laughter brought tears to his eyes. Eddie's shocked face soon crumbled as she joined him.

"Don't worry, Coach. We won't tell a soul."

"Hey, Coach, how can we help?"

"Want us to help?"

Twelve eager young girls crowded around Add and Eddie

with offers of help and suggestions for revenge. Add noted each one, discarding most but filing a few away for possible use in the next few days.

An hour later, Eddie shut the door on the last giggling teenager and sagged against it, eyes closed, exhaling an exhausted breath. She had just enough strength to open one eye and survey the disaster that constituted the remains of the victory party.

Paper plates and soda cans lay tumbled every which way atop each inch of counter space. Condiment jars, half empty and slathered inside and out with the drying remains, littered the top of the kitchen table. Ice cream bowls with sprinkles, chocolate, caramel and who-knows-what filled the sink. And the floor! Mud covered most of it, some dried, some still damp enough to be a travel hazard.

She closed the lone eye and sighed.

"Good party," Add said softly, tempting her lips with a fleeting kiss before he began collecting the disposables.

"Why do good parties always look like a war was fought and lost?" Eddie asked, savoring the taste of his kiss for a long moment.

"If people are enjoying themselves, they don't notice the mess they're making," Add said. He dumped a load into the compactor and twisted the on button.

"This was a good party?" Eddie asked, ferreting out a dish-rag buried under the bun bags.

"This was a *fantastic* party," Add assured her, taking the rag from her hand and guiding her to a chair.

She didn't protest when he pushed her into the seat and lifted her legs to rest on a second chair. Rolling her neck on her shoulders to relieve the last of the stress, she watched as Add efficiently cleaned all of the refrigerator jars and stowed them away.

"My God! What happened?" Charles roared, pushing the swing door from the dining room open and stopping dead in his tracks.

The muscles in Eddie's neck began to knot again even before

she turned to face the other couple standing dumbstruck in the doorway. She had to gulp back the laugh that threatened when she noted their incredulous faces.

"You two missed one fantastic party," Add said, bumping the refrigerator door shut with his hip as he tossed the dishrag in the general direction of the sink. "Hot dogs, relish, home-made ice cream." He lifted the kettle full of hot dog water to carry to the sink.

Chloe, in a simple but elegant silk dress, stepped cautiously into the room behind Charles. Her carefully created eyes were large and horror-filled as she inspected the room.

"*Incroyable,*" she gasped, twitching her skirts away from the tower of used paper plates leaning crazily on the counter nearest her. "Have you called the police? Was anything damaged?"

Add and Eddie stared at her before exchanging glances and shrugging.

"Edwina, since it finally appears you've completed your day's work, I must insist we discuss the disposition of the house," Charles began, stepping carefully around the mud in the middle of the floor. He brushed off a chair seat with an unused napkin before sitting down at the table.

Eddie peered at him, her forehead creasing in a frown as she tried to concentrate on his words. "Now?" she asked wearily, reaching down to unlace her shoes and pull them from her feet. She sighed with pleasure as she yanked off her socks and wiggled her toes.

"You weren't available today or this evening. You seem to have a very busy schedule," Charles explained coolly. He pulled a sheaf of papers from the inside pocket of his jacket and sought a clean place on the table to spread them out. "I think now would be an excellent opportunity."

The kitchen clock interrupted her reply. She counted ten measured beats as she tried to hold in the temper threatening to erupt.

"Charles, I truly want this matter settled as much as you

do,'' she began, dropping her bare feet to the floor and resting her hands on her knees. "But I still have papers to grade before tomorrow's classes and . . . '' She swung her arm out, encompassing the muddy floors, the littered table, and dirty counters.

"Surely you can set this aside for the moment,'' Charles began only to be stopped by a furious scream.

Chloe remained by the door as Charles approached Eddie and seated himself at the table. She viewed the well-honed muscles under Add's snug T-shirt with a speculative gleam. She watched avidly as they tensed when they took the weight of the large kettle.

"That must be very heavy,'' she purred, sidling up to Add and drawing one poppy-red nail down his arm from shoulder to elbow.

"Very,'' he told her curtly, moving toward the sink as quickly as he could without sloshing hot water over himself.

"You do not mind?'' she asked, flicking manicured fingers toward the mess on the counters. "Doing women's work?'' Her hand circled his arm, testing the muscle.

Add glanced toward the table in the corner. Charles was intent on his conversation with Eddie and totally oblivious to anything else in the room as he pulled papers from his suit coat.

"Work's work,'' Add returned, careful to maintain a neutral tone and resisting the urge to shake off Chloe's hand.

"Do you lift weights?'' she asked softly, sliding her hand across his shoulders.

"Nope.'' He lifted the kettle, setting it near the edge of the counter beside the sink.

"Such definition,'' Chloe said with a sigh.

Add tried to ignore the fingernail she dragged tantalizingly up his neck to his ear. He managed to evade her questing fingers by leaning forward to empty the sink. The minute he straightened to stack the ice cream bowls on the counter, she was there again, gliding her hand across his shoulders and over his back.

The muscle at the edge of his jaw jumped as he ground his teeth together and managed, barely, to maintain a polite smile. Just as he lifted the kettle once again and began to tip it, he felt her fingers slip inside his pants.

Chloe shrieked in outrage as the cascading water from the kettle ricocheted from the bottom of the sink and drenched the counters and her hair, make-up, and expensive silk dress. Nothing escaped the greasy water spraying wildly from the sink.

Add thumped the kettle down on the counter and turned to confront a bedraggled, sputtering Chloe.

"Imbécile! Bouffon! Saccade!" she screeched, pushing a drooping wave from her eyes.

"Hey, I'm sorry," Add said, his tone almost penitent as he reached for the dish towel on the rack nearby.

Chloe filled the air with harsh, guttural French, jerking the towel away from Add.

Charles was at her side in an instant, his tone soothing as he grabbed a fresh towel and tried to blot up the moisture. She slapped furiously at his hands. Hovering at her side, Charles scowled at Add.

"What have you done to my wife, you cretin?"

"No harm intended. I was just emptying the kettle. Darn thing was pretty slippery." Add shrugged.

Eddie's arm circled Add's waist and she leaned around his chest to get a better view of Chloe. Her fingers clutched tight as she swallowed the shout of jubilation that bubbled inside her. Her lips were compressed in a tight line as she met Add's eyes.

"Soak that dress in cold water," she offered hesitantly, afraid if she said too much she'd burst into laughter.

"Cold water? This is a Chanel original!" Chloe spoke scath-

ingly, hurling the towels to the floor and shoving Charles away
from her. ''The gown is ruined.''

The rest of her fury was vented in French as she stomped
from the room, leaving a trail of greasy water behind.

Charles fixed his gaze on the ceiling for a moment before
glaring at the two in front of the sink and then striding from
the room.

Eddie couldn't control her laughter a moment longer.

''Did you see . . . ''

''I didn't know . . . ''

Eddie released Add to wipe the tears from her cheeks and
tried to cast a stern, no-nonsense look his way. She failed
miserably when she noted the water dripping from his greasy
spiked hair, his nose, his eyebrows. She couldn't help it. She
laughed again, folding her arms about herself to ease the stitch
in her side.

Add continued chuckling as he began to mop up himself and
the counter.

''Was it an accident?'' Eddie asked, grabbing a towel of her
own to wipe the cupboards dry.

''I can't exactly say,'' Add replied, dropping his towel to
the pile on the floor and beginning to slide the whole soggy
mass around to soak up the rest

''Why not?'' Eddie picked up the towels and wrung them
out in the sink while waiting for Add to explain.

''I *think* I'm a better person than to do that deliberately.''
He swiped up more water from the floor and handed the dripping
towels to Eddie.

''Then how?''

Add slid his eyes toward Eddie and grimaced. ''Chloe.''

''Chloe dumped the water on herself deliberately?'' Eddie
frowned, totally bewildered.

''No.'' Add's tone was hesitant, the single word drawn out
to almost three syllables. He concentrated on the towels held
in his clenched fists.

"Addison Rivers. What happened?" Eddie demanded, stunned when she saw bright crimson flood Add's face.

"She grabbed my buns and I jerked." His face grew dark with embarrassment.

"Chloe?" Eddie asked incredulously. *"Mon chère? Amante?* Charles' *wife* grabbed your buns?"

"If you dare laugh, Edwina Mason, I'll tell the entire school your middle name. No, the entire town," Add threatened, hurling the last of the towels into the sink.

Eddie swallowed the laughter that had bubbled up before it could be born, her eyes growing rounder and rounder as she waited for the teasing gleam in Add's eyes that didn't come.

"You wouldn't. You couldn't," she tried bluffing. "You don't know it."

Slowly Add smiled, wicked highlights streaking into his dark eyes. He just watched Eddie, his smile growing bigger as she grew more unsure and began backing away.

"Would you?" she asked, her tone unsure.

Add considered her question, drawing out the suspense of the moment until she was ready to scream.

"Guess I can't," he finally said, grinning at the sigh of relief that escaped her. "You didn't laugh, Edwina Hermione."

Add shooed her off under protest to grade papers while he cleaned up the kitchen. By the time she rejoined him, papers graded, the disaster area was again her sparkling kitchen, right down to the floor. Arm in arm they headed for their bedroom.

Before Add was finished in the shower, Eddie was sound asleep. He watched her for a moment, taking pleasure in viewing the gentle rise and fall of her breasts beneath a Raiders sleep shirt. When a third yawn escaped him in as many seconds, he dropped a tender kiss on her forehead and found his pallet, now with an air mattress beneath the coverlet, and was out almost before his head hit the pillow.

* * *

Eddie tossed her book bag to the floor near the foot of the stairs as she entered the house and headed for the refrigerator and the cool lemonade waiting there. She came to an abrupt halt when she saw Charles, clipboard and calculator in hand, kneeling on the floor inspecting the underside of the dining room table.

She was tempted to tiptoe into the kitchen for a moment's peace and quiet but she ignored the temptation. Sooner or later she had to face the man, like it or not.

"Lose something?" she asked, stooping to peer beneath the table, too.

"Umph," Charles exclaimed, knocking his head on the underside of the table as he began backing out.

Eddie straightened and, with her hands on her hips, waited.

"I was just checking to see if there was a manufacturer's mark anywhere," Charles explained, smoothing his hair as he stretched his neck uncomfortably above his raw cotton shirt.

"Why?" Eddie asked, smoothing a wrinkle in the tablecloth that protected the surface.

"Knowing the manufacturer will help me date the piece and therefore establish a price for it," Charles told her, making a quick note on his clipboard.

Eddie frowned and turned toward the kitchen. It probably would have been better to slip in for the lemonade without disturbing Charles, she told herself. If he was thinking what she suspected, the headache that had been threatening all morning was about to erupt into a full-out migraine.

She pulled the pitcher from the refrigerator, and waved it at Charles. "Would you like some?"

Charles took a seat at the table and begin flipping pages before answering her. "Yes, that would be fine."

She reached for two of the 'recycled' glasses she used most of the time and froze. The cupboard that normally held three shelves of tightly packed glasses was nearly empty.

Her glance shot to the sink that had been blessedly empty this morning thanks to Add's efforts last night, only to find it piled high with glasses, plates, and pans. The overflow was piled haphazardly across the counters. From the looks of it, there couldn't be much left in any of the kitchen cupboards.

Scowling at the mess she knew she'd have to clean up before supper tonight, she took down two glasses and tipped the lemonade pitcher. Three drops plopped into the glass. She shook the pitcher experimentally and removed the lid. Empty.

She opened the freezer to look for more concentrate. Her knuckles turned white on the handle as she confronted the chaos that had once been neatly stacked, serving-size packages of meats and vegetables. *Whoever,* she wouldn't even think the name, had plundered the freezer. Once neatly wrapped and labeled bundles were shoved every which way, the paper around them torn to expose hamburger patties and chicken breasts.

Cans of frozen juice concentrate rolled forward as she tried to straighten the jumble, hitting her shoulder and chest before she could dodge them.

"She-e-e-et," she shouted to the ceiling, using the mutated swear word again and again while she tried to force the freezer door shut.

"Is something wrong?" Charles asked, still ruffling through his papers.

"Is something wrong!" Eddie yelled, rounding on Charles. "Look at my kitchen! Do you see anything wrong here?"

Charles stared blankly. "There isn't any reason to raise your voice."

"I'll raise my voice if I want to," she cried, waving her arms wildly about while striding from one end of the room to another, lifting and discarding one dirty kitchen utensil after another. "What have you done to my house?"

"Our house," Charles returned, his voice a bit testy. "This is *our* house."

Eddie froze, a carving knife clutched in her hand. Lizzie Borden's rhyme ran through her head.

She laid the knife gently on the kitchen counter, careful to move it back from the edge precisely three inches. *No court in the land would convict me, not under the circumstances,* she told herself while her fingers fisted at her sides. If only she hadn't just finished redoing the cupboards, if bloodstains were easier to bleach out of wood . . .

She cut off the thought and began counting. She didn't even slow the steady rhythm when she reached ten. Twenty slipped past almost unnoticed. By the time she hit forty she had synchronized the count to her breathing. At sixty she began to draw her fingernails one by one from the flesh of her palms. Although she wasn't exactly calm by eighty, she had accepted what couldn't be changed.

"Will the lemonade be much longer?" Charles asked from the table.

Her only response was the heavy thump of her hand against the kitchen door as she escaped before she did her former fiancé permanent, irreversible, physical damage.

Chapter 7

The bedroom door shook the entire house as Eddie slammed it with every bit of pent-up rage that boiled within her. Her actions were jerky as she dragged the band from her hair and shook her head.

"Just be saccharine sweet and hang on my every word," she grumbled to herself as she paced the room.

"They'll be gone in three days." She mimicked Add's voice and jerked a wrinkle from the bedspread in passing.

"Well, they're not gone and I'm tired of being sweet." She finished another circuit of the room, wishing for something to destroy. Finding nothing she was willing to sacrifice, she made straight for the bathroom and the shower to cool off.

She wasn't only furious, she was hot and sweaty from a day spent teaching with no air conditioning and an afternoon baseball practice in a broiling June sun. By the time she reached the bathroom door, she had her T-shirt off and her hands on the placket of her shorts. Her hands froze at the sight in front of her.

Towels were thrown everywhere, not one having found the hamper near the door. Puddles covered the tile floor. She swore like a sailor when she took a step into the room and slid, stopping only when she met the opposite wall.

Fearfully, she looked toward the sink. Perhaps a little cold water on her face would help prevent the nervous collapse she knew was imminent. There was no sink, at least not that she could see. The countertop, which only this morning had seemed so generous, was littered with every possible cosmetic known to humankind. *Not only is there every type, there's got to be every brand of every type,* she thought, dropping to the toilet seat.

It took a moment before she could gather her courage and peek behind the shower curtain and into the tub. It was amazingly, startlingly, wonderfully empty.

"Okay," she said to the room at large, squaring her shoulders as she rose. "I'll take a shower. I'll get cool. I'll relax. Maybe while I'm behind the curtain the bathroom fairies will clean up this mess."

She reached for the door to the linen cupboard and pulled it open. Nothing. There was absolutely nothing in it. She stood on tiptoe to check out the top shelf. When she couldn't see anything, she shoved her hand in and scrabbled across the empty shelf.

"She-e-et," she screamed at the room, slamming the cupboard shut and stalking into her bedroom.

Grabbing her sweat-stained T-shirt from the floor, she jerked it over her head and yanked her hair free of the collar. She stomped about the room, mumbling under her breath and snatching discarded pieces of clothing from the bed, chair and floor before returning to the catastrophe that had been her bathroom.

Calling down curses on every person not adult enough to pick up after themselves, she dragged the hamper through her bedroom to the hall.

"Thank you, God, for the small things," she mumbled as she stopped at the door to the laundry chute, and began pushing things down.

Without breaking stride, she left the bedroom again and headed for the basement. She refused to look anywhere but at the door to the basement when she hurried through the kitchen. If she considered this mess on top of the other at the moment, she just might pick up the knife that lay exactly where she'd left it on the counter.

Charles lifted his head as she entered the room. He even opened his mouth as if to speak. One glance at her stormy expression had him burying his head back in his papers, his fingers rapidly punching numbers into his calculator.

Eddie clattered down the worn wooden stairs.

It didn't take long to stuff the washing machine with towels and set the dials. She checked her watch before heading back up the stairs. If she wanted a shower anytime before midnight, she'd have to remember to run back down and toss everything into the dryer in an hour. By then maybe she'd be able to find the counter in her bathroom again.

She didn't even glance in Charles' direction as she passed through the kitchen on the way back upstairs. He didn't try to get her attention this time either. *Good thing, too,* she thought, *or I'd have told him off.*

Surveying the cosmetics that littered the bathroom counter, Eddie swore there couldn't be a thing left on the shelves in any drug, grocery, or department store in Hendricksburg. Maybe even Columbus. Thank heavens she'd experienced the cramped chaos of dorm life, or the task ahead would have terrified her.

First she transferred all of her things from the drawers on either side of the sink to a shelf in the linen closet. Then she attacked the jumble of tubes, jars, bottles, brushes, and assorted paraphernalia Chloe had left.

Each of the various facial areas was assigned a drawer on either side of the sink along with the combs, brushes, picks, lifters, pins, ribbons, barrettes, and bows grouped in the first drawer. Hair curlers—hot, moist, and dry—curling irons, and blow dryers. Finally, in the last drawer, she placed what probably belonged to Charles. His razor, mousse, sprays, deodorants and colognes were almost as assorted as Chloe's.

By the time she shoved the last bulging drawer closed, she was still faced with the containers too large for the drawers. Wondering how one lone woman could use so much stuff, she dug through her closet until she found a mirrored tray. Placing it on the bathroom counter, she stacked the tall cans and bottles by order of size on top of it.

Eddie checked her watch and headed for the basement to throw the towels into the dryer and collect the mop and some rags so she could attack the general mess that remained. By the time she had scrubbed the tub, sink, and floors it was time for the towels to come out of the dryer.

Her step was a bit slower as she headed downstairs with her cleaning supplies and absolutely dragging when she headed back up with a basket of clean towels. *The end is in sight,* she reminded herself as she turned down the hall for her bedroom.

"What have you done?" Chloe demanded from the bathroom as Eddie entered the master bedroom.

Eddie dropped the basket of towels on the bed before she turned to the bathroom, praying all of her work had not been undone.

Chloe's heavy French accent combined with her outraged shrieks as she strode about the small room waving her arms, made the words nearly unintelligible.

"What have I done with what?" she finally asked, leaning against the door jamb for support.

"My things. My *cosmétique.* Where are they?"

"Why were they here in the first place? I thought you had a dressing table in your room, Or is this just the overflow?" she questioned, her voice rising slightly in anger.

Chloe gave a Gallic shrug and waved the question aside like a pesty gnat. "I could not pull out the bench. The room is much too small. Besides, the light is better here and it's more convenient."

Convenient for whom? Eddie wondered and took a deep

breath, trying to hang onto a sense of calm that was quickly slipping away. *Nothing will be served by returning fire,* she told herself. *If you get in a shouting match with Frenchie you may never get to the shower.*

Eddie struggled to hold onto her I'm-the-teacher-and-I-will-be-calm voice. "*I've* put things away. You'll find *your* things in the drawers grouped by their use," she explained in the soft voice her students would have instantly recognized as deep trouble.

Chloe did not. She gave no attention to the slender woman standing stiffly in the bathroom door but continued her tirade. The tight smile on Eddie's face that drew her lips thinner and thinner with each passing second totally escaped her notice.

"How dare you?" Chloe ranted, yanking open the drawers and pawing through the contents.

"Stop right there," Eddie commanded, advancing into the room, her eyes darkening in outrage. "If you touch one thing in those drawers you'll find every last one of your precious pots of goop in the compactor."

Eddie shoved the top drawer shut with her hand, nearly taking Chloe's fingers in the process.

"I've spent the last two hours finding *my* bathroom and I'm not about to let you undo all my work." Eddie punctuated her sentence by ramming the second drawer shut. "If you and Charles expect to stay here, you'd better learn right now that I am not the maid."

The third drawer was driven home. "If you don't like where I've put things, take them to your room, or should I say rooms?"

Eddie kicked the bottom drawer shut and advanced on Chloe, shoving her index finger at the woman and backing her from the room. "Right now I'm going to take a shower. I prefer to do that alone so I suggest you leave or I may just have to toss you out on your French *derriére.*"

By the last word, Eddie had Chloe in the hall and the slamming door punctuated the end of the sentence.

Eddie leaned wearily against the bedroom door, listening to

Chloe crying Charles' name as she ran down the stairs. Taking a deep breath, she blew it out slowly amazed at how energized she felt after her outburst.

Before pushing away from the door, she flipped the lock then sauntered to the bed and claimed two of the thickest towels in the basket. Humming softly, she went into the bathroom and turned the water on full force in the tub after adding a generous handful of lilac-scented crystals to the water.

Seconds later she sank into the fragrant bubbles, a paperback in one hand and a spongy foam pillow in the other.

Add settled his broad shoulders against the door frame and enjoyed the view of Eddie, oblivious to his presence, reclining in the giant claw foot tub. Her head was pillowed against the back edge, her hair draping over it to fall nearly to the floor. Her rounded shoulders peeked now and again from waves she created with one tapping foot. Gripped in her slender fingers just above the water was a book that held her rapt attention, its pages crackling as she turned them impatiently.

He took a long drink from the glass he held. It should have cooled him, but it didn't. He wanted to step back, into the bedroom, but his legs wouldn't respond. He tried to picture Eskimos cocooned in fur from head to foot but instead his mind gave him images of Eddie, her golden tan arms and legs contrasting vividly with her pale breasts and belly. He felt a familiar stirring in his loins.

Taking a deep, calming breath, he struggled to gain control of his libido. Half of him wanted to move into the room and improve his obstructed view, but he hesitated to take that final step. What he glimpsed now, in the privacy of her bath, while a torch to his desires, was no more than he could see on any public beach, less in fact. But to take that final step would be an invasion, a taking, and that wasn't what he wanted, what he craved with Eddie.

And if you ever hope to succeed, you'd better cool it now, he instructed himself sternly, gulping down the last of the lemonade. His forced his mind to conjure up her image in thirty years, hair gone white, crow's feet about her eyes, but the image was still wearing one of the silly cotton night shirts she favored. His groin tightened painfully.

Forcing what he hoped was a teasing grin to his face he asked, "Has he kissed her yet?"

Eddie squealed and dropped her paperback. Water splashed over the edge and onto the floor as she slumped beneath the rolled rim of the old clawfoot tub then turned and dragged herself snugly against the side, sending more water cascading to the floor.

"Look what you did," Eddie howled, waving the sodden paperback in the air while clutching the side of the tub with her free hand.

"He didn't kiss her yet?" he asked politely. "Did they . . ." Leaning against the door jamb, he lifted his empty glass and waved it around then grinned and waggled his eyebrows suggestively.

"O-oh!" Taking aim, she let the book fly. The soggy mass plopped onto the floor just beyond the bedroom door, missing him completely when he ducked. Eddie ground her teeth in frustration.

"How did you get in here?" Eddie demanded, scrabbling around the bottom of the tub for the washcloth she'd lost.

"Old locks are easy to pick," Add explained, tipping his glass to lick the melted ice cubes. "My brother and I did it all the time when we were kids."

"That's breaking and entering," she sputtered. "You turn around and get out."

Add just grinned.

"Now!" Eddie shouted, lifting her arm slightly from the water, her fingers squeezing some of the water from the washcloth.

"But, sweetheart . . ."

The words weren't out of his mouth before Eddie sent the

cloth hurtling through the air and then clasped the tub edge with both hands.

"Hey," Add croaked as the washcloth caught him full in the face, sending water flying and drenching the front of his uniform shirt. Snatching it before it could plop to the floor, he tossed it up and down in his hand, his smile growing dangerous.

The minute Eddie noted the golden lights flashing in his eyes she knew she was in trouble. Her gaze darted wildly about searching for the towel she'd absently dropped when she'd got into the tub. It lay in a heap on the end of the vanity counter, just out of reach unless she were to rise from the water.

Following the direction of her glance, Add set his empty glass down and grabbed the towel, wiping the water from his face and hair before draping it over his shoulder while still playing catch with the wet washcloth.

"How long have you been in there? Are you pruny yet?" he asked. "Aren't you cold?"

The suggestion made goose bumps prickle along Eddie's exposed arms and back as the barely tepid water sloshed around the tub. She couldn't hide the chill that shook her when the breeze from the window set high above the tub whispered across her exposed shoulders.

"Yes, I'm probably pruny," she said, her lips beginning to tremble with cold.

"Don't you think it's time you got out?" he asked in feigned innocence. The washcloth went plop, plop, plop in his hand. "They're asking for you downstairs."

The reminder of what had sent her here in the first place almost made her sink beneath the water, never to rise again.

Watching her eyes roll toward the ceiling in divine supplication, Add couldn't help teasing, "Charles was quite concerned. Wanted to come up and check on you himself." For good measure he added, "Chloe thought perhaps she could help by starting dinner."

The threat of Chloe on the loose in the kitchen was almost enough to make Eddie jump out of the water, but the sound and feel of the sloshing water around her reminded her quickly enough that she was totally naked.

"Over my dead body! Give me the towel and go away so I can get out," she said crossly.

Add considered her request for a moment. "I could," he finally said, pulling the towel from his neck and dangling it just beyond her reach. "What will you bribe me with?"

Eddie growled low in her throat and cupped one hand just below the level of the water. Add took a step back and frowned.

"Okay, okay. I was only teasing," he told her, swinging the towel toward the tub.

"Just drop it and leave," Eddie directed, scowling up at him but still clutching the tub.

"Spoilsport," he called over his shoulder as he tossed her the towel and headed for the door. "By the way, you still have nice buns, Mason," he added just before the closing door cut him off.

Eddie was out of the tub and had the towel draped around herself almost before the door clicked shut. She pulled the tattered robe she now shared with Add from its hook behind the door to wrap around herself.

She really should be furious with Add for spying on her, she told herself as she let the water out of the tub. But she felt a grin tease the corners of her mouth.

She leaned back against the door and glanced toward the tub as the familiar gurgle told her it was empty. How could she be mad at a man who was so much fun?

The answer was simple. She couldn't. Besides, despite his teasing remarks and his stunt with the towel, he couldn't possibly have seen anything from where he'd been standing.

Anyway, who but Add would spend time in a room with a naked woman trapped in a bathtub and not take advantage of the situation? *A man who had no interest in the naked woman,* her mind answered depressingly.

Closing her eyes, she rested her head against the door. Why should the thought of Add having no interest in her naked body depress her? Charles had obviously lost all interest in her and that didn't depress her. She was angry and hurt by his defection, but not depressed.

Pushing away from the door, she peered at her reflection in the mirror.

She twisted and turned, examining what shape could be seen through the tattered terry robe. Figure acceptable. After all, Add *had* said she had nice buns. Eyes bright. Skin clear. Teeth good. Well, she had no apparent physical flaw, she decided, picking up her brush and pulling it through her long, and healthy hair.

Was there some other flaw that made her undesirable to men?

"Men!" she muttered to herself. She tossed the brush onto her shelf in the linen closet and slammed the door. "Totally illogical, incomprehensible fools. Forget about them."

With a sharp nod of agreement for her mirror image, she yanked open the bathroom door.

Chapter 8

Eddie didn't hurry to dress. She sorted carefully through her closet, matching a pale blue T-shirt with dark blue walking shorts, and scrabbling in the bottom of her closet until she found a pair of blue deck shoes.

She returned to the bathroom and arranged her hair, sweeping it back from her face with a pair of antique gold filigree combs she'd found at a yard sale. With a gold barrette that could have been part of the set, she collected her long waves at the nape of her neck.

Make-up came next. Mascara and eyeshadow to deepen the green—but subtly, until an Irishman would have thought himself with the angels. She ignored blusher. The confrontation with Chloe that awaited her made it was unnecessary.

Pleased with her appearance, she took a deep, fortifying breath and emerged from her bedroom. She could hear faint voices from the lower floor and allowed herself a small smile at the outraged flurry of French and English.

"Offensive, not defensive," she whispered to herself as she headed down the stairs.

Her sneakered feet were silent as she crossed the hardwood

floors toward the kitchen door. She stopped for a moment, her hand on the door, gathering her courage.

"Bearding the lion in his den?" The soft words were whispered next to her ear.

She whirled around to face Add.

"Where did you come from?" she demanded. "What do you think you're doing sneaking up on me like that?"

"I wasn't sneaking around," Add offered with a shrug. "I was waiting for you. It was worth it," he finished, inspecting her from top to toe.

Eddie could feel a blush creeping into her cheeks and she couldn't meet his glance. Anticipating his arm around her shoulders any moment, she tried to brace herself against the tremors his touch always evoked.

"Well, do I pass?" she asked, a bit testily.

"With flying colors," Add answered. His arm circled her waist and he placed a tender kiss against her temple.

Eddie wanted to melt into his embrace, but the strident voices from the kitchen reminded her of her purpose. She was here to settle Charles's beef, not be loved up by Add.

She looked up at Add. "Come with me?"

Add's arm tightened around her, encouraging her resolution while his hand covered hers on the kitchen door.

"Wouldn't miss this for the world," he answered with a soft chuckle. He pushed the door open.

Together they marched into the disaster area that had been a kitchen, toward Charles and Chloe who stood rigidly beside the table. Deep spots of color flamed in Chloe's cheeks as she glared at them. Charles's left eye began to twitch as they drew closer.

Eddie forced herself to ignore the disorder about her and concentrate on the other couple. Her own arm now circled Add's waist.

"You wanted to talk, Charles," she began. Slipping from Add's arms, she moved around the table to the chairs nearest the windows before taking a seat. "Let's talk." She clasped her hands in a tight knot on top of the table.

Add nearly choked on suppressed laughter when he finally saw the motif on the front of her T-shirt.

Careful detailing left no doubt that the house depicted on the shirt was Eddie's. Blazoned across the sky-blue background just above the chimneys was the logo, *Mine, All Mine.*

Grinning from ear to ear, he took the seat next to Eddie's and wrapped his tanned fingers about her slender hands.

Charles sputtered, his eyes bulging as he read the words screaming at him from across Eddie's chest. His knuckles turned white where he clenched the ladderback chair before him. He jerked away from the manicured fingers that grasped his shoulder.

"What is that supposed to mean?" he croaked, his finger pointing toward Eddie's T-shirt.

Eddie plucked the T-shirt away from her body and scrutinized the picture. She met Charles' furious gaze and shrugged. "It was a gift from my students. Didn't they do a marvelous job? The house is absolutely perfect."

Add turned the hoot of laughter caught in his throat into a cough as his hands tightened around Eddie's. She ignored him, tilting her head and watching Charles' face go from crimson to near purple with outrage.

"Not the house," he shouted, lifting the chair and thumping it back to the floor.

"They thought 'home, sweet home' was too saccharine," she explained calmly. "They believe in a more materialistic approach."

"Are these words supposed to mean something to us?" Chloe asked. She took the chair next to her husband and waved at the offending shirt.

"Oh, that," Eddie said with an easy chuckle. She smoothed imaginary wrinkles from the front of the shirt and ended with an affectionate pat on the image of the house itself. "This house has always been referred to as the Eastons', even when the Humphreys and Thompsons lived here. After we finished the outside renovations and got it all painted, people decided it wasn't the Eastons' anymore, that's all.''

Eddie's innocent explanation and guileless expression finally drove Charles to collapse into his seat at the table. Clutching his clipboard in both hands, he scowled as Chloe whispered frenziedly in his ear, her French running together until it all sounded like one long, drawn-out word to Eddie.

Crossing her legs at the ankle, Eddie drew one hand free of Add's to straighten the lace doily centerpiece of the table. With meticulous care, she fluted the edging until it stood up independently. Satisfied with the improvement, she wrapped her hand around Add's arm, leaning against him before blowing softly into his ear.

He hugged her arm close to his chest and bent to whisper in her ear. "You are one bad woman," he said, taking a moment to tease her ear with his tongue. "Remind me never to cross you."

"Oh, Add," she answered with a giggle, just loud enough to draw the attention of the couple opposite them. The moment she knew they were watching, she tilted her head and met Add's lips for a quick kiss.

"If we aren't interrupting," Charles began loudly, glowering at the two as he struggled to regain his composure. He smoothed the notes on his clipboard and proceeded. "Perhaps we could discuss the expenditures you've made during the past year, Edwina."

Eddie stared into Add's eyes, mesmerized by the sparks of gold that kept shooting through the deep chocolate brown. *I shouldn't have kissed him,* she told herself while struggling to look away. *I will not kiss him again,* she thought. *At least not right now.* With a sigh she forced herself to face Charles and ignore Add's fingers wandering up and down her back.

"Yes. Expenditures," she repeated absently.

"I have a list here of the things you detailed in your letters,"

Charles began, rifling through the papers on his clipboard. "Are there any additions you'd like to make?"

"Probably. I've got the canceled checks in my office," she replied.

"I'd like to see them. I need a detailed accounting completed before we come to a final figure, but with the down payment of $7,500.00 and other expenses which we will split fifty-fifty, I believe a figure of $10,000.00 to buy out your share of the house and furnishings would be reasonable," Charles said bluntly. He finally had Eddie's full attention.

"Buy out my share?" Eddie said, the quiet, no-nonsense teacher voice she'd used earlier on Chloe in evidence once again.

"We discussed this briefly the day Chloe and I arrived," Charles explained in a calm voice.

"And I explained that I don't wish to sell my house," Eddie returned, equally calm. "Nor do I wish to sell any of *my* furniture."

Charles grunted loudly when Chloe nudged him in the ribs. With a sideways glance toward his wife, Charles spoke again.

"I'm sure we can reach an acceptable figure. If ten thousand doesn't seem enough, perhaps we could agree to some compensation for the time and effort you put into the decorating as well."

Add leaned back in his chair the moment he felt the muscles tense across Eddie's back. He looked at the couple opposite as he folded his arms across his chest and waited for the fireworks to begin.

Eddie laid her hands precisely on the table and rose, her eyes never leaving Charles's face.

"I don't wish to be compensated for decorating *my* home. I don't wish to share expenses for renovating *my* home. I definitely don't wish to sell *my* home," she said softly, her cheeks flushing deeper with each statement. "However, I will give some thought to what I might owe you for negotiating the purchase."

Charles and Chloe stared aghast at Eddie as she pushed back her chair and walked around the table. Charles jumped to his feet, knocking over his chair as he reached out to grab her arm and twirl her around to face him.

"What do you mean?" he growled, pushing his brick-red face close to hers.

Eddie tried to shake off his hold, but his fingers dug deeper into her arm.

"*My* savings went to make the down payment for this house. *My* salary for the past year made the mortgage payments. *I* paid the utilities. *I* paid for the repairs that turned a dump into a home," she ground out. "I'm not about to walk away and let you have it all."

With a last furious jerk, she reclaimed her arm and stepped out of reach before firing her final salvo. "And *I* kept it neat and presentable. If you intend on remaining here as a guest, clean up your mess or, deed or no deed, I'll have you arrested for trespassing."

She turned on her heel and stomped from the room, totally unaware of the Cheshire cat smile that lit Add's face as he stood and sauntered after her. One hand on the kitchen door, he turned back to Charles, standing speechless at the table.

"I wouldn't put it past her," he said, shaking his head in wonder and turning toward the door only to turn back. "Maybe you should know, it was Eddie who talked the police chief's son into staying in school and tutored him to bring up his grade point. That man would do anything for her."

Add turned and followed Eddie out.

"Hey, wait up," Add called, letting the screen door slam shut as he charged down the porch steps after Eddie. He followed at an easy jog as she marched down the street, arms swinging in cadence with her feet.

He smiled when he heard her mumbling to herself.

"He said they'd be gone in three days. Three days my great-aunt Fanny! They won't be gone in thirty-three days or a hundred and three days. They're entrenched. They'll probably drive me out first.''

Add didn't interrupt, allowing her to vent her fury. He stayed at her side, grateful every step of the way that he was accustomed to healthy exercise because the pace she set would kill anybody else. In silence they covered two miles in near record time.

Eddie didn't notice Add at her side. A red haze filled her mind, blocking out everything but the fury that burned through her. She didn't notice her students who waved as she passed. She didn't even notice her breathing become labored at the rapid pace she'd set until a stitch clawed at her side and she had to stop at the grassy knoll just inside the park.

Bent over from the waist, she rested her trembling hands on her knees and inhaled one quavery breath after another.

''Great speech,'' Add said, dropping to the grass beside her and taking her hand at last to pull her down. ''Greater work out.''

Eddie fell back full-length in the grass and stared up at the sky turning dusky blue as the sun headed for the distant horizon.

''Competing in any marathons?'' Add asked, reclining next to her.

''No,'' she said, still slightly short of breath. ''Think I should?''

''No, you've got enough to worry about.''

Their conversation died and they lay in the ensuing silence watching the setting sun streak the sky with pastel hues.

''Do you think I went too far?'' Eddie asked, pushing the hair that had escaped from her side combs away from her face.

Add captured her hand before it could drop back to the ground.

''Well, did I?'' Eddie demanded impatiently. Her fingers closed tightly around his larger hand.

''Why? Isn't it all true?'' he asked, stalling her.

''Yes.''

"Then you didn't go too far," he answered, drawing her hand toward his lips.

Eddie watched Add pull her index finger into his mouth and swirled his tongue tantalizingly around the tip. Her breath caught in her throat when he ever so slowly drew it back out.

Crickets chirped merrily away, counting out the degrees of temperature as Eddie and Add lay side by side. Only their hands met, twining and separating, while their breath grew short and their eyes clouded.

"Addin' up strikes with the Coach?" a voice called from a passing bicycle, shattering the bubble that had enclosed them.

Add met her eyes. Her dreamy, confused glance almost pulled him back to the enchantment that had spun out between them. The shout of a mother and the disappointed reply from her child reminded him of where they were at long last.

"Ice cream," Add said forcefully, bounding to his feet and pulling Eddie after him.

"Ice cream?" she asked in confusion.

"Ice cream," he answered with a determined nod as he tugged her toward the street lights and the vendors' wagons beneath them.

Eddie allowed him to lead her toward the lights. She didn't resist him, although she thought she wanted to. Her skin tingled pleasantly although somewhere in the haze of what had been her brain she thought she probably shouldn't be enjoying the tingle as much as she was.

She took the cone he shoved into her hand, her tongue sliding around the peak to capture the drops that were already melting and racing away. She peeked at Add from between her lowered lashes, imagining sampling the spot of ice cream his tongue had missed on his own lips.

She pushed the thought away. Now, when they were headed for her home, her bedroom was not the time to consider the emotions churning inside her. She'd made a terrible mistake before in her choice of men. If she allowed her heart, battered and bruised as it was, to set her course now, there was no telling what greater folly she could commit.

No, now was a time for drawing back, being cautious. If her feelings for Add were real, they'd still be there after she'd mended. After she'd recovered a degree of sanity. And she'd broken all ties with Charles.

And if he cared for her, really cared, beyond simple friendship, beyond momentary lust, he'd still be there. She hoped so with all her heart.

Eddie, book bag in hand, headed for the den off the living room. With a mass of papers to grade, she didn't need the distraction of Charles' constant questioning of what she'd paid for everything in the house. No matter what her personal problems, she wasn't about to shortchange the kids who were taking her summer course.

She bumped open the door with her hip. It swung wide and she took two steps into the room before she stopped dead. There, seated at her desk, going through every drawer, sat Charles.

"What do you think you're doing?" Eddie demanded, dropping her bag to the floor and striding across the room. Charles withdrew another folder from the drawer before he sat upright and turned to Eddie.

"You said you had receipts collected in here and since you've been so busy with summer school and the baseball team, I thought I'd take care of the task myself," he explained, opening the file on the desk top.

"These are my personal papers. You have no right to go through my things," Eddie stormed, reaching for the folder.

"How are we to determine the current value of the house if we don't have an accurate accounting of the additional expenditures?" he asked in a reasonable voice, moving the folder just out of her reach.

Eddie took a calming breath. She wouldn't win any points

if she sounded like an hysterical fool. "We don't need to know the current value of the house," she explained finally.

"Of course we do. To determine a reasonable buy-out figure, we must know what additional funds have been expended." He continued reading the papers in the file and slowly turning them over. Occasionally he made notes on his ever-present clipboard.

"There won't be a buy-out," she fired back, forgetting her resolve to remain calm the moment Charles implied she'd be giving up the house. "I have no intention of giving up my home to you."

"You're not thinking logically, my dear," Charles explained, closing the folder and turning toward her. "I'm fully aware of the salary you're making. This house, with its mortgage payments and repair bills, is putting a great strain on you even with your new husband. Chloe and I are prepared to free you from the responsibility. Of course, we wouldn't consider letting you walk away without proper recompense for your time and effort."

Drawing herself up straight, Eddie retorted. "It didn't seem to bother you over the past year that I was handling the mortgage payments and repair bills single-handedly. Oh, I forgot, we were engaged then."

"It was a shared responsibility, Edwina. You weren't shouldering it alone," Charles said calmly, stacking the folders he'd been perusing in a neat pile on his clipboard.

"I wasn't? You could have fooled me," she fumed, her hands on her hips as he turned the chair to face her. "I don't recall seeing a single penny coming from you that would suggest *sharing the responsibility.*"

Charles pushed the chair away from her and rose to his feet. "Edwina, you know I explained that living in Paris took every penny of my fellowship money."

Eddie advanced. "Oh, yes, living in Paris. If it was so expensive, where did you find the money to woo your little wife?"

"In the early stages of our acquaintance, we were often

guests at the same functions. Chloe's father is the head of the Economics Department and she often accompanied her father or served as his hostess,'' Charles explained, his left eye beginning to narrow while the tips of his ears took on a more crimson hue. ''When we realized we were becoming more than acquaintances, I explained my situation to her.''

''How did you explain me?'' Eddie demanded, advancing a step toward Charles. ''Or didn't you tell her about the little fiancé back home?''

Charles's face became mottled as he struggled to maintain a cool front. ''As acquaintances it didn't seem imperative,'' he began, brushing imaginary lint from his sleeve.

''And later on I really didn't matter,'' Eddie finished for him.

''Good Lord, Edwina, what was I supposed to say? Her father was in charge of my fellowship,'' Charles retorted, taking a step back.

''And we couldn't possibly do anything to anger her daddy, now could we?''

''You know the academic world. Earning an advanced degree is dependent upon the good opinion of your superiors.'' Charles circled Eddie to pick up his clipboard and the files he'd removed from her desk.

''Well, I know the world of toads,'' Eddie said, following Charles and grabbing at the files under his arm.

The files slipped from Eddie's hands, scattering across the floor in a blizzard of paper. Dropping to her knees, she began gathering them up. She rose and faced Charles.

''In the toad world, you made a promise to share a life with me and fix up this house. But toads don't keep promises.'' She stepped away so Charles couldn't get the files. ''Well, I keep my promises. I promised to fix up this house and I did. I promised to pay the bills and I did. I kept my side of the agreement, and now I intend to keep my house.''

''My name is still on the deed as an equal owner,'' Charles protested.

"That means you may be entitled to half of the down payment, maybe," Eddie grudgingly acceded. "But I've got proof that that's all your participation amounted to. I'm not going to give up this house because you and your new wife have decided you want it."

"Then I guess we'll have to settle this in court," Charles blustered, his tone not quite as assured as it had been.

Eddie paused. If Charles learned she wasn't married to Add, he could hurt him terribly. She didn't want that to happen, but she just couldn't hand over her home to him either.

"If that's what you want," Eddie agreed, lifting her chin a notch higher.

Unable to shake her determination, Charles turned on his heel and marched from the room, slamming the door in his wake.

Eddie collapsed onto the desk chair, the files cradled in her arms. It took several minutes before she was able to relax enough to sort them into the proper folders again. Satisfied at last, she took all of her papers from the desk drawers and shoved them into the bag she carried to school each day. There was no way she was leaving them where Charles could get his hands on them. For all she knew, he might make them disappear if he had the opportunity.

Chapter 9

Chloe, dressed in a slim-fitting linen suit, sat in the fake leather chair and crossed her legs. She looked around the room the receptionist of Holmes Realty had ushered them into and turned to Charles. "How soon will these people be able to sell the house?"

"First we've got to get Edwina to consent," Charles pointed out, strolling about the small office and checking out the magazines on the table in the corner. "I believe she'll be amazed how much the house has appreciated over the last year. Once she understands that she's made a profit, I doubt she'll continue arguing."

"What if the little fool refuses to sell? I will not live in that house indefinitely," Chloe stated firmly. "No closets, sharing a bathroom with strangers. How do you expect me to entertain your colleagues in such a place, not to mention having those little *bourgeois* idiots stumbling through?" She threw her hands in the air.

"We won't be living there long, *mon chère*. Edwina doesn't like open confrontation. She'll soon crumble if we suggest legal action,'' Charles assured his wife, coming to her side and patting her shoulder.

''And what of our visit here today?''

''There's nothing wrong with seeking information from someone knowledgeable,'' Charles assured her. ''It's not as if we've actually sold the house without her consent.''

''Could we do that?'' Chloe asked, a gleam of pleasure lighting her carefully made-up eyes.

''Not legally.''

''Could we offer it for sale? Once we have a buyer, would she be so quick to turn away from money in hand?''

''It might not be wise to move too quickly,'' Charles cautioned, turning to walk back to the window that overlooked the parking lot.

''Perhaps, but perhaps a *fait accompli* would be to our advantage,'' Chloe said, shaping her lips into a practiced smile as the office door opened.

''Hope I haven't kept you waiting long, folks. Not good to keep clients waiting, you know,'' the reality agent said as he sailed into the room, a folder clutched in his left hand. ''I'm Al Crocker and you must be Mr. and Mrs. Whitney. What can I do for you folks today? Have a seat, have a seat.'' He pumped Charles's hand and then Chloe's before rounding the desk and reclining in the oversized desk chair.

''We'd like to discuss the possible sale of a home I own here in Hendricksburg,'' Charles began, pressing the knife-sharp crease in his pants with his fingers.

''What's the address?'' Crocker asked, grabbing a pen from the set on the desk and making a note in the folder spread before him on the desk.

Charles gave him the address and answered the numerous questions that followed in meticulous detail. Finally Crocker laid his pen aside and beamed on the pair before him.

''So you're interested in selling?'' he asked, flashing a toothy grin at them. ''I hope you aren't planning on leaving our little community?''

"Not at all," Charles explained, glancing at Chloe for a moment. "I bought the house before I met my wife and before I accepted a position at the University."

"Bachelor days. Most new wives don't want their husbands reminded of bachelor days. I know Mrs. Crocker didn't," he expounded. "Once we were married, we sold my place and got one that was more to her tastes."

"Precisely," Charles said. "My wife is French and American Victorian doesn't suit her sense of style."

"Ah, you're French. I thought I heard an accent," Crocker enthused with a nod for Chloe. "The French have a unique style. I believe I have a house that might be just what you're looking for. A bit more upscale. Just what a university professor would appreciate. Perfect layout for entertaining," he gushed, drawing a folder from the pile on the side of his desk.

"How lovely," Chloe answered, tipping her head graciously. "But at the moment, we are only interested in the home my husband owns."

"Of course, of course. Before you can buy a new home, you must know what's to be done with the present one." Crocker said with an agreeable nod. "I'm familiar with the neighborhood your house is located in. If I'm not mistaken it's the old Easton place. Charming, charming house."

"As you say," Chloe answered, shifting in her seat and baring another two inches of thigh. "It has a certain charm, but I'm afraid it is not in my style."

"A woman's home should be an extension of her personality," Crocker agreed affably.

"*Exactement*," Chloe answered, lifting the corners of her smile just a bit. "You do understand."

Charles coughed, drawing Crocker's attention back to him. "Our future plans will, of course, depend upon the sale of this house," he pointed out.

"By all means. Let's concentrate on the home you have," Crocker hurriedly agreed. "The first thing we'll need is an appraisal. You've made some really wise improvements this past year. That ups the price.''

"Of course," Charles said, his tone condescending.

It didn't take long to arrange a time for Crocker to appraise the house when Eddie wouldn't be there.

"I'd really hate to have you make a second trip down here just to sign papers," Crocker added, pulling a set of forms from his ever-present folder. "Why don't you just sign the commitment papers now and save a trip later?"

"Commitment papers?" Chloe said, her French accent very thick as she glanced toward Charles.

"Nothing to worry about. They simply give Holmes Realty exclusive rights to sell your home. This way the company doesn't have to charge a fee for the appraisal." He went into detail about the figures that marched down the right side of the form. Sliding the papers across the desk and laying a pen on top, he added, "Most of these costs will be passed onto the buyer at the time of sale. Of course, if you just want an appraisal, my office does have to charge a fee. That's to protect our time expenditure in the event you decide to sell through another agency."

Charles glanced toward Chloe, noting the feral gleam in her eye. "Might my wife and I have a moment to discuss this?" Charles asked, lifting the papers and running his gaze quickly down the neatly typed pages.

"Certainly. Certainly. My secretary has some papers for me to sign," Crocker said, rising and moving toward the door. "Take all the time you need."

Chloe was out of her seat pacing the room almost before the door clicked shut. "There is nothing here to consider. Unless we want to pay that little man for his services now, we must sign the papers agreeing to let him handle the sale."

"It would appear so," Charles agreed, watching Chloe cross back and forth in the small office.

"Even if these papers are signed, it does not mean we have

to sell the house, *non?* It just means we agree to let these people sell it if we sell," Chloe pointed out as she resumed her seat.

"It would appear so," Charles returned, beginning to read the contract more carefully.

"Then there is no question," Chloe said, taking the pen and passing it to Charles.

Minutes later Crocker returned. "Have you come to a decision?"

"My wife and I are in agreement, Mr. Crocker, that your agency should have the rights to the sale of my house," Charles said firmly.

"Let me call in my secretary to witness the documents and we'll have you folks out of here in no time," he exclaimed, beaming across the desk at them while summoning his secretary.

With Crocker and his secretary hovering at his shoulder, Charles accepted the pen held out to him and quickly signed the papers.

"And now your lovely wife," Crocker said, passing the pen to Chloe.

Without a moment's pause, Chloe accepted the pen and signed the papers.

Crocker looked them over briefly before passing them to his secretary for her signature. "Edwina doesn't sound like a French name," he commented, as he took the papers and slipped them into his folder.

"It is a family name," Chloe answered quickly, rising and slipping her purse strap over her shoulder. "Quite *ancien.*"

"And you're keeping your maiden name?" he asked, rising from behind his desk.

"I had my wife's name added to the deed before we were married," Charles quickly filled in, also rising and offering his hand. "There hasn't been time to have the original deed altered at this point and it did seem senseless if we're going to sell."

"Quite reasonable," Crocker said, shaking Charles's hand

and then reaching for Chloe's. "I'll be out Monday to do the appraisal then."

"We'll be expecting you about ten," Charles said, his hand on Chloe's elbow as they headed for the door.

Beaming and waving vigorously, Crocker watched them climb into the red Mercedes before heading back into his office rubbing his hands gleefully.

Eddie slipped in the back door, her shoes in her hand. Flinching when the click of the latch echoed through the kitchen, she turned and stared in amazement about her. Pristine counters sparkled in the afternoon light from the windows. Not a pot, pan or coffee cup was to be seen. Even the floor shone.

Apparently someone had taken her outburst the other night to heart. She probably shouldn't have been surprised to find the kitchen back to normal. When she'd gotten back from the ball game last night, the bathroom had been neat and clean, exactly as she'd left it after her wild woman cleaning spree.

Maybe she should explode more often, she thought with a grin, inspecting the refrigerator and its neatly filled racks. If all it took to get people to pick up after themselves was an explosion, she'd begin stockpiling dynamite tomorrow.

Still half afraid of what might be hidden away, she slowly opened the cupboards nearest her. Plates, cups and glasses marched in orderly rows across the upper shelves. Pots and pans were stacked neatly by size below.

"Whoever, I thank you," she whispered, afraid if she spoke out loud her housemates would descend on her. She hadn't seen any of them, except for a sleeping Add, since the night she'd confronted Charles and Chloe about the house. Coward that she was, she'd slipped out the front door each morning before they were up.

Morning classes, afternoon ball practice and last night's game had filled the hours and enabled her to avoid them all. She'd extended her reprieve even more with a pizza party for the team after they'd won last night's game. By the time she'd gotten home, everyone had been sound asleep.

Of course, she hadn't managed to avoid them on her own. Charles had taken his poor darling wife out to dinner that first evening after she'd dropped her bombshell and run off. With Add gone by four-thirty each morning and asleep by the time she got home, she hadn't had to face him either.

Eddie peeked around the side of the dining-room door. She breathed a sigh of relief when she found the rooms beyond empty. She paused for a moment at the bottom of the stairs, listening intently for any sounds that might alert her to the presence of anyone else in the house. Things were blessedly still.

Her foot was on the first step when the telephone rang. She grabbed the phone from the maple secretary beside the stairs by the fifth ring.

"Hello?"

"This is Al Crocker of Holmes Realty. Is Mr. Whitney available?" Eddie's eyes darkened when the caller identified himself.

"No, Mr. Whitney isn't available right at this moment," she said, crossly. "May I take a message?"

"Sure. Would you tell him that I've got the figures from the appraisal? I'd like to drop it off, along with his copy of the letter of commitment, at his earliest convenience."

Eddie stared at the wall for a moment, absorbing the meaning behind the caller's words. Charles had gone behind her back and was planning to sell the house. *How dare that little weasel!* she fumed to herself.

"Miss?" The voice on the other end of the line drew her attention.

"I'm here," she said, taking a deep breath and making her voice even and calm. She had to derail things until she had time to think. Her brain worked furiously, searching for an excuse that sounded plausible.

"Mr. Whitney was called out of town unexpectedly. He said he'd be gone about a week," she explained.

"That's too bad. Is Mrs. Whitney available?"

"No, she accompanied her husband."

There was silence on the line for a moment. "Since you're obviously house sitting for them, would it be possible to show the house anyway? I've got some prospective buyers already."

"I don't think that would be a good idea. They left me to finish some remodeling in the bedrooms and with stripped wallpaper and floor sanders making such a mess . . ." she left her explanation hanging and prayed he'd accept it.

"I see. I see. Probably would be best to wait until you're finished. The fresher and snappier a home looks, the easier it is to sell and the higher price we can get for it."

"I'm sure." Eddie waited. She could almost hear the man's brain grinding out schedules and figures over the line.

"How about I call Mr. Whitney by the end of next week, and see how things are going?"

"That would be fine, Mr. . . . ."

"Crocker. Al Crocker of Holmes Realty," he supplied quickly.

"Mr. Crocker. I'll be sure Mr. Whitney gets your message."

Eddie clutched the phone in her hand for several minutes after the realtor hung up. She'd bought some time, but how much, and what was she going to do if Charles tried to follow through with the sale?

She climbed the stairs and leaned wearily against the bedroom door.

She yawned, her jaws popping as the yawn grew wider and wider. Perhaps she'd just take a short nap before the others got home. Just a few minutes to revitalize, she thought, collapsing on the bed and pulling the throw over herself. Her eyes drifted shut.

There were twenty tests waiting in her bag to be corrected before tomorrow's class. She yawned again. Well, maybe just a few minutes. Her mind would be clearer and the grading would go much quicker.

She snuggled beneath the throw and took a deep breath, inhaling the woodsy, smoky scent Add favored. It was almost like having him hold her in his strong arms as he had the evening on the grassy knoll at the park. That had been pleasant. No, more than pleasant. Wonderful. Her lashes settled on her cheeks and didn't rise again.

"Oh, yes. Yes," Eddie moaned in her sleep sometime later. She shot upright in bed. Her glance searched the shadows in the room. There was no one to note the flushed color that tinted her cheeks or the rapid rise and fall of her breasts. She took a calming breath. She *was* alone. But the dream had been so vivid, so . . . so erotic.

Good lord. what's wrong with me, she wondered, brushing sleep-tangled hair from her eyes. Mere days ago she'd been madly in love with Charles, anxious for his return, planning her wedding, and now she was dreaming about Add, wanting to make mad, passionate love to him. Was she fickle? Was she suffering from a previously latent overactive sex drive? *That's a laugh,* she told herself without humor. She'd hardly have waited a year to entertain thoughts about Add if she was.

The memory of Add Rivers' deliciously tempting lips had been appearing in the strangest places. When she glimpsed a billboard, she found his smile shining down on her. While lecturing her class, she could lick her lips and taste the citrusy, smoky, sultry essence of him.

As if imagining such things wasn't bad enough, she was kissing him at the drop of a hat. Surely real newlyweds weren't so demonstrative in public. And she was responding to his touch like some sex-starved virgin.

Well, she admitted to herself, dropping back onto her pillow, *that wasn't far from the truth.* Charles had been her first lover, but only after they were engaged. Even then she'd not succumbed with such enthusiasm, such total loss of awareness of everything else in the world that one kiss from Add could cause.

She tried again to remember the way she'd felt when Charles kissed her, fondled, her, made love to her. The only image that surfaced was Add. His tanned legs stretched across her porch steps. His well-muscled shoulders straining under the weight of her new bathtub. How his eyes darkened just before his lips met hers.

Try as she might, she couldn't remember even Charles' kisses. Had they been soft, firm, moist, dry? She remembered only the fullness of Add's lower lip, the soft texture of his tongue, the citrusy taste of him. She had to fight an hysterical giggle. Of course he tasted citrusy. Most of the times they'd kissed were after they'd been drinking lemonade.

Good lord, she had it bad. She'd lived with Charles for a year and couldn't remember anything about him. Just seeing Add, awake or asleep, was enough to start her heart racing and her skin tingling in anticipation of his touch.

Were the hormones she'd ignored for the past year totally out of control? Was anyone in pants that dared cross her path going to become an object of her desires? She moaned in despair.

Was poor Mr. Thompkins next door safe? The image of the 71-year-old grandfather, his bald head gleaming pink beneath the summer sun, served to bring a twitch of a smile to her lips. No, Mr. Thompkins at least was safe.

Why Add? Was it because he was her friend and therefore safe to place in her fantasies? Because he was under 50? Because he was there? *He's a nice guy, offering support during a difficult time,* she grumbled to herself. *And all you can think about is jumping his bones.* She threw her arm over her eyes. What would he think of her if he found out?

She'd turned his life upside down because she was afraid to face Charles alone. What a rotten way to repay Add's friendship. After he'd teased and cajoled her out of her bouts of loneliness and come running whenever some crisis with the house had been beyond her ability, she was fixating her hormone overload on his unsuspecting head without any regard for what he might want.

She'd become a manipulator just like Charles.

Okay, Edwina, she told herself sternly, *it's time to get a grip.* She'd taken her fifteen minutes of self-pity. Now it was time to begin fighting for what she deserved. Her house. Shoving her libido back into the closet where it had lain dormant the past year, she slammed the door firmly shut. When she was free, house and all, of Charles's taint, she'd explore whatever might be possible with Add. In the meantime, she had to clear her house of unwanted guests.

Her stomach growled. How long had it been since she'd had something to eat, she wondered, sitting up on the side of the bed. Pizza last night? How could she make plans when her stomach protested so loudly? Flinging the throw aside, she rose and headed for the kitchen.

Chapter 10

"Hey, long time, no see," Add called, dropping his mail pouch beside the door when he entered the house. "How goes it?"

Eddie turned a tentative smile his way. "I'm still here," she said, ignoring the fluttering of her heart. "But so are Charles and Chloe."

Add took a glass from the cupboard and filled it from the pitcher in the refrigerator before leaning back against the counter and letting his eyes feast on Eddie. He noted the violet smudges beneath her eyes with concern. Apparently, she wasn't sleeping any better than he was.

"Heard you won another game," he offered in an attempt to keep the conversation light.

"Ten to three," she said distractedly.

"Bet the girls are in seventh heaven."

"They were pleased," Eddie answered, resting her hands on the edge of the sink and turning to Add. "They were far more interested in 'the plot.' "

"What plot?"

"You, me, Charles, Chloe," Eddie explained, a flush tinting her cheeks. "They're calling it 'the plot,' as if it were one of Trish Peterson's mother's romance novels."

"Have they decided who gets the girl?" Add asked, a sly grin tipping the corners of his mouth.

Eddie's blush deepened. "You, of course."

"Any mad, torrid, passionate kisses?"

Eddie's face took on the shade of over-ripe tomatoes before she stammered out, "Hundreds, until we discover we were meant for each other and fall madly in love. Of course, in the meantime, we all but destroy the house in wild attempts to get Charles to leave."

"Any workable ideas?"

"How do you feel about living with Samantha?" Eddie asked, smiling.

Add frowned in concentration. "Samantha? Did I have her in a class?"

"Not unless you subbed in science," Eddie said, her eyes beginning to twinkle.

"The kid only takes science classes?" he asked, his brows lowering.

"Samantha is that snake Mrs. Fuller is so fond of," Eddie finally supplied.

"That ten foot monstrosity that almost escaped into the ceiling?" Add demanded, his voice cracking in horror.

"That's the one."

He shook his head adamantly. "I'll stick with Charles, although if you don't mind Samantha . . . I could go to a mailman's convention for a few days."

"No way are you leaving me alone in this house with Samantha, Charles and Chloe," Eddie fired back. "They'd probably kill her and leave me to explain to Mrs. Fuller."

"Well, it was a thought," Add said. "Any other suggestions short of wild animals in the living room?"

"Not at the moment, but give me time. Of course, we could always burn down the house," Eddie replied, blowing stray hairs off her face as she went back to work on the potato in her hand. "No, way too drastic. What worries me is the parents getting wind of what's going on here." A worried crease etched deeply into her brow. "We could lose our jobs."

"I doubt the girls are going to run home and tell their parents," Add assured her, squeezing her shoulder.

"I know that," Eddie said. "But if their parents overhear some of the plots they're dreaming up, we could go to jail for contributing to the corruption of minors."

Add decided it was time to approach their major problem head on. "What *do* you want to do about Charles?"

"I'm not sure what to do," Eddie answered thoughtfully, dropping the peeled potato she'd been working on in the pot beside her and reaching for another.

"I don't have any proof it was my money that made the down payment. Maybe we should have had one of those . . . those pre-wedding agreements," she said, dropping another potato in the pot and starting on the next.

"Those things seem like an admission of defeat before you even get into the game," Add replied, stealing a cookie from the jar.

"Maybe so, but it would have made everything simpler now," she said with a shrug while wiping her hands. "At least my name is on the deed. I guess I should be thankful for that."

"You've got your canceled checks to prove *you* paid the mortgage and for the repairs," Add reminded her, taking an appreciative sniff of roasting meat when she opened the oven door. "That ought to give you some leverage."

They lapsed into silence as she basted the meat and put the potatoes on to boil. Add took plates from the cupboard and began setting the table for four.

Eddie took a glass of lemonade to the table and sank into a chair. "Leverage isn't enough," she finally blurted out. "I can't afford to go to court any more than I can afford to buy him out. Every penny I've got is tied up in this house. Besides, if I go to court it will come out about . . . you know . . . us."

"So, you'll borrow from me."

Eddie stiffened at the suggestion before shaking her head. "I'd be right back where I started, owning the house with someone else who could take it away from me and with a lot more reason.''

"Then that settles it," Add returned evenly before taking the seat beside her.

"Settles what? How?" she fired back.

"We'll have to go to plan B."

Eddie scowled across at him. "How do we go to plan B when we didn't even have a plan A?"

Add waved her question away and sat grinning at her, waiting patiently for her to ask the next logical question.

"Okay, I give up. What's plan B?" she asked when she could stand the suspense no longer.

"We drive them out," Add explained, taking a sip of lemonade.

"Wasn't that supposed to happen after we gave them a room with no furniture and no closet?"

"That would only stop the faint of heart and Charles has no heart to be faint of."

"So?" Eddie prompted him.

"Remember when the plumbing backed up?"

Eddie nodded with a grimace, remembering the mess it had left behind. But she'd had that fixed and she wasn't about to unfix it and face that kind of monumental clean-up just to discourage Charles from claiming her home. Confusion darkened the glance she sent Add.

"And the furnace failed?"

She nodded while her eyebrows rose in apprehension. That had been horrendous, no heat in January with 20 degree weather, but this was June, late June, and one of the warmest in years.

"How about super glue on the toilet seat?" His eyes sparkled wildly and her heart skipped a beat.

"Dries too fast," Eddie pointed out. "Unless, of course, you have a burning desire to lay in wait under the bed until one of them needs to make a visit."

Add shook his head. "Not me. You'd think after dealing

with hundreds of teen-agers we'd know every stunt in the book designed to drive an adult nuts.''

"We probably do, but we don't want to drive them nuts. We want to drive them out.''

They both gave serious thought to possible nondestructive pranks.

"What if they think the repairs you made were strictly cosmetic? I doubt Charles would be quite so enthused about dumping this house on a buyer who'd sue his pants off for nondisclosure,'' Add finally suggested.

"Like what?'' Eddie asked, the smile from their earlier silliness leaving her face as she considered the possibilities.

"If the shower head were to fall off any time the water was turned on. Would Charles know enough about plumbing to doubt us when we told him the pipes needed to be replaced before a permanent fix could be made?''

Eddie considered before shaking her head. "I did most of the plumbing when we were together. He might believe you.''

They lapsed back into silence for a time.

"You know he wants the furniture, too,'' Eddie told him. "I still haven't gotten around to replacing that spring in the wicker couch in the living room.''

"If we took the board out . . .''

"They'd sink like everybody did when I first got it,'' Eddie finished for him, capturing the spirit.

"Then there're the renovations.''

The worry lines in Eddie's face cleared a bit. "Are you sure they'd notice the mess?''

"Depends,'' Add answered, a slow grin tipping his lips upwards. "When do you think we can rent the floor sander?''

Eddie's face brightened and a light of comprehension began to sparkle in her eyes.

"Not until after we strip the wall paper and refinish the woodwork,'' she answered, getting into the swing of things.

"I wonder how Chloe is at stripping?'' He ducked the punch Eddie threw his way. "I meant woodwork.''

"I'm sure you did," Eddie returned with a knowing smirk. "Stripping will damage her nails though."

"If Charles and Chloe want to claim half ownership of the house, it's about time they started helping with the fix-up."

"It does sound reasonable," Eddie agreed, getting the lemonade from the refrigerator to refill their glasses.

"How is Charles with kids?" Add asked, and cocked his head at the sound of car doors slamming in the driveway beyond the windows.

"Terrible," Eddie answered quickly, remembering his reaction to Tommy. "Why?"

"With the house expenses, you can't go entertaining and rewarding your team with pizza twice a week," Add pointed out.

"True."

"It only seems right that you entertain them in your home. Perhaps a slumber party if they win the conference would be nice," Add suggested, warming to his topic.

"Or a barbecue after Saturday's game."

"Do they paint?"

"Probably every bit as well as Chloe," Eddie answered cheerfully.

"Then a paint party is a must. We wouldn't want to work Chloe too hard."

By the time Charles and Chloe entered the kitchen, their fellow newlyweds were toasting each other with lemonade.

Eddie stretched, her arms high over her head and listened to the sounds of mourning doves just outside her bedroom window. She took a deep breath, sampling the sweet scent of roses mixed with the sharp pungency of marigolds that wafted through her open bedroom window. Ah, Saturday morning. It was almost worth the five days of teaching it took to get here.

Shoving aside the sheets, she threw her legs over the side.

"Argh!" came a deep-voiced complaint. Her feet had made

contact with Add where he lay stretched on the air mattress at the side of her bed.

She jerked down her nightshirt, and climbed over him before remarking, "Time to get up, sleepy head. It's yard sale day."

His only response was a groan as he pulled the pillow over his head.

"I'll take first turn in the bathroom," she called out just before shutting the door.

Add pushed the pillow away once he heard the door click shut. Extending his arms over his head, he moaned when he discovered several new muscles that were unhappy about the current sleeping arrangements. *And that's not the only problem,* he thought with a sigh, pushing himself to a sitting position on the floor.

It was pure hell sharing this room with Eddie, sharing the nights with her, engulfed by the lilac scent she wore, touched by the same gentle breeze that brushed against her. He'd tossed and turned half the night trying to push thoughts of her scantily clad body from his mind. He hadn't succeeded very well. Once he'd fallen asleep, she'd haunted his dreams.

Pulling the sheet about himself, he stood and stumbled to the window, trying to forget the sight of her long, sleek legs as they had reached over him just moments ago.

Usually he had all day walking street after street on his mail route to gain control of his baser instincts, but today he had no escape. When Eddie'd proposed a day of yard sales to get them out of the house and away from the dynamic duo, he'd agreed.

"You must have a death wish," he muttered to himself as he took a pair of battered jeans with frayed holes in the seat from the drawer Eddie had allotted him in her dresser. Jerking a shirt from the closet, he leaned against the wall next to the bathroom door to await his turn just as the sound of the shower ceased.

He inhaled slowly, forcing himself to stare at the Buddha Eddie had picked up at a yard sale. Maybe if he concentrated on that, he wouldn't think of Eddie, naked in the shower, water sluicing over her full breasts, down her slightly rounded stomach to slip down and around her pelvis just where he'd like to run his fingers.

He shook his head. There probably wasn't a thing in the world that would succeed in driving her from his mind.

"May I come in?" Chloe's voice coming through the panels of the bedroom door finally brought his wayward mind crashing back to reality.

"Just a moment," he called, swathing himself in the linens from his improvised bed. With a quick glance around, Add opened the door a crack and peered at Chloe standing in the hall.

Every hair lay in perfect order on her head. Her face was picture perfect, her pouting lips full, sexy and expertly painted. Her eyes were lazy-lidded and inviting as they surveyed his sheet-draped figure.

"*Bon matin,*" she said, her voice low with implication. "I see I have awakened you. This I did not expect."

"It's Saturday," Add mumbled, tugging the sheet more securely around him.

"Your day off," Chloe returned, resting her hand on the door. "How nice that you will have time to spend with your little bride. Or perhaps she is engaged for the day?"

Add ignored the blatant offer in her voice. "Yeah, it's *our* day off. Did you need something?"

"I did not wish to intrude but ... the bathroom," she answered. "There is only one shower and one door to it."

"Eddie's in there right now," Add offered, leaning against the door to prevent Chloe pushing it further open. "We shouldn't be much longer. We've got plans."

"Too bad that you have plans. It might make things easier for all of us if we could spend some time together," Chloe suggested with a lift of her eyebrows. "Perhaps Charles and I could accompany you?"

"I doubt you'd enjoy it," Add said, glancing over his shoulder and praying for Eddie to come to his rescue. "We're going to some yard sales. See what treasures we can find."

"Yard sale?" Chloe asked, leaning against the door frame and crossing her feet at the ankles so her robe split open to reveal a shapely leg to mid-thigh. "What kind of treasures do they sell at these yard sales?"

"People clean out their houses and things they don't want or can't use any more, they sell," Add explained with another yank at his makeshift toga. He held back a sigh of relief at the sound of the bathroom door opening. "Your junk could be my treasure. Eddie can probably tell you more about them. I just go along for brute strength."

"Magnificent brute strength," Chloe whispered, catching sight of Eddie just over his shoulder. *"Bon matin,* Edwina."

"Chloe," Eddie answered stiffly, ducking under Add's out-stretched arm. She kissed him quickly on the cheek, her arm around his waist before she faced the other woman. "Bathroom's all yours, sweet cheeks."

Add balanced her chin on his fist and met her lips for a breath-stealing kiss. He had to wait a moment before he could speak. "I won't be more than five minutes, sweety."

With a nod for Chloe, he bolted into the bathroom.

"Addison says you are going shopping," Chloe said, peeking over Eddie's shoulder until the bathroom door clicked shut.

Eddie shrugged her shoulders. "In a manner of speaking."

"Perhaps I would enjoy this shopping, too."

Eddie forced her voice to an even tenor. "I don't think so. Everything's secondhand. Kind of like hand-me-downs."

"What are hand-me-downs?" Chloe asked as she surveyed the cut-offs and T-shirt Eddie wore with disdain.

"Things somebody hands down to you after they're done with them," Eddie explained, putting a saccharine smile on her lips. "Rather like marrying someone else's fiancé, I guess."

Chloe inhaled sharply at the insult. "No, I don't believe I would be interested in your hand-me-downs. It would not appear to have any challenge. Not at all like going after what one wants and winning against others."

Eddie seethed silently as Chloe turned on her heel and marched down the hall. She slammed the bedroom door just as Add exited the bathroom.

"Don't tell me she's going yarding with us," he complained, buttoning his shirt as he came all the way into the room.

"No, she's not," Eddie fumed, jerking the covers on the bed far more forcefully than was necessary to straighten them. She pummeled the pillows before tucking them under the bedspread. "There's not enough *challenge* for her French palate."

"She's never faced you over a piece of furniture you really want," Add assured her, grabbing her hand and heading toward the door. "The woman obviously doesn't recognize a killer shopper when she's face to face with her."

Add didn't allow her time for a response, barely pausing long enough for her to grab her purse from the corner next to the door where she usually dropped it. In seconds, they were down the stairs and headed out the front door. The roar of his van as they backed from the driveway was their only farewell.

Eddie surveyed the spare bedroom Monday afternoon. The faded red plush wallpaper was dark and depressing. The room would look twice as big when she took it down. She flipped the borrowed steamer on and began her assault on the walls.

She didn't see Chloe leave her room and head for the bathroom. The hiss and groan of the motor on the powerful tool blotted out the scream that followed shortly afterwards. When the little engine stopped abruptly, she finally looked up.

Outlined against the far wall, waving the plug in her hand, stood a bedraggled Chloe. Water dripped down her face, spotting the silk dressing gown that covered her reed-thin body. A small puddle was already forming on the floor at her feet.

"What happened?" Eddie asked, fighting not to laugh at the woebegone figure.

"The shower ... the thing with the water ..." Chloe growled, her French accent making it hard to understand the garbled words. Lifting her hand, she thrust the shower head at Eddie. "It attacked me. Look what it has done to me."

"Oh, yeah, it does that sometimes. I hope it didn't hit you,"

Eddie said matter-of-factly as she set the sander down and walked toward her nemesis.''

"Hit me? It ruined my hair. I spent two hours at the hairdresser and look at it. How am I to appear in public like . . . like this? I must attend a very important luncheon today and look at me."

Eddie had to bite the inside of her cheek to keep from grinning. "Want to borrow my hair dryer? My hot curlers and curling iron are in the linen cupboard in the bathroom, if they'd be any help," she offered, widening her eyes innocently.

Chloe sputtered for a full minute before taking a deep, calming breath. "You told Charles you had the plumbing fixed." She waved the shower head wildly, nearly striking Eddie in the temple.

"I had the toilet fixed. It kept spewing stuff back at me," Eddie said, with a gentle shudder.

"Spewing?"

"Spitting. Erupting. Sometimes it was like a crazy volcano."

"And why have you not had this fixed?"

Eddie took the shower head from Chloe's hand and headed for the bathroom. She called over her shoulder. "Do you have any idea what plumbers make an hour? It's not hard to fix."

Chloe was right on her heels as she entered the bathroom and pushed the shower curtain aside. Standing on tip-toe, she screwed the part back into place. "It was cheaper to just tighten it once in a while. The plumber suggested we might have to replace all of the pipes in the house to fix this. Something about threads wearing out," Eddie explained and stepped back, wiping her hands on her cut-offs.

Waving her arm like some game show host presenting a prize, Eddie said, "Ta-da. Good as new."

Eddie hurried away and returned to the other bedroom. She didn't see Chloe's eyes narrow belligerently at her retreating back. Once she had plugged in the steamer and turned it back on, she allowed herself to laugh. Humming a tune she'd heard on the radio that morning, she went back to work.

Chapter 11

Eddie flipped the switch on the steamer to off and pushed damp tendrils of hair away from her face with her shoulder before reaching out to see if the wallpaper was ready to start peeling.

"Lemonade break," Add called from the door, two large chilled glasses in either hand.

Eddie made her way cautiously toward the door through the clutter of tools and refuse that littered the floor. Taking the glass Add offered her, she drained it before rubbing the moisture-beaded side across her forehead, down her cheeks and around her neck.

"Where're your helpers?" Add asked.

"Meeting at the University."

Add joined Eddie on the floor. "Chloe teaching there, too?"

"Faculty wives' tea," Eddie explained.

Add nodded his head knowingly. In the two weeks since they'd proceeded with their plan to finish the renovations, every excuse known to man had cropped up to delay Charles' and Chloe's participation. If it wasn't meetings and teas, it was getting ready for them. To date their housemates hadn't stripped, steamed, or cleaned one inch of faded wallpaper.

"It's too hot for you to be working up here," he said, taking a hefty sip from his glass.

A warm June had turned into one of the hottest Julys on record in Ohio. Rain had become a memory of spring long past. Even the grass had opted to turn brown under the water conservation restrictions the town had set up.

"This is the last wall to do in here." Eddie mopped her face and neck with a bandanna. "As soon as it's done, I can sand the floors down and start the fun stuff."

"Painting in 95 degree heat without air conditioning or fans is not going to be fun stuff," Add pointed out, refilling her glass. He watched the rise and fall of her breasts beneath the faded, cropped T-shirt that molded them so lovingly.

It was a struggle to drag his eyes away from the damp V that showed her cleavage and directed his gaze toward the clearly-defined nipples at the center of each rounded globe. His hands burned to hold them, feel their weight. He rubbed the beaded side of the lemonade pitcher across his own forehead. The pitcher blocked the enticing view but it did nothing to cool the heat rising in his groin.

"Maybe there'll be a breeze," Eddie offered, fatigue clear in her voice as she pushed to her feet and went in search of her putty knife.

Add shrugged out of his own T-shirt and found a knife of his own under a pile of crumpled paper. He joined Eddie, and slid his knife carefully up the wall, watching her from the corner of his eye.

Each time she reached toward the top of the wall he held his breath, wondering if the cropped T-shirt she wore would reveal a glimpse of her breasts. He had to swallow his disappointment time and again when her arm came down to the bottom of the work area to begin again.

They worked on in silence until the wall was free of paper. Add took a deep breath and blew it out slowly, trying to contain his disappointment. Whoever had designed those tops Eddie wore must be a mathematical genius. That's what it would take to figure out how long to cut the stupid things without cutting them short enough to satisfy a man's fondest dreams.

Eddie stepped back and surveyed the wall, checking carefully for any spot that might have been missed. Satisfied the wall was as clean as peeling could make it, she set her knife aside and picked up a piece of sandpaper. With graceful strokes, she began sanding a lump.

Her breasts jiggled beneath her shirt, and her bottom, just visible beneath the ragged fringe of her cut-offs, wobbled with each movement. Torture to watch for the man who shared her room but not her bed.

Add groaned beneath his breath and grabbed the sandpaper from her hand. "You sweep up the mess. I'll do that," he said, taking his frustrations out on the wall.

He ran his hand along the wall, checking for rough spots and wishing it could be Eddie's slender back beneath his questing fingers. He threw himself into smoothing each bump as if his life depended on it because his sanity certainly did.

He froze when he caught sight of her curvaceous backside as she bent over and collected a pile of scraps from the floor. He closed his eyes, his breathing shallow, and tried to think thoughts of Alaska, the Antarctic, anything that would cool his libido. Nothing worked. His thoughts turned the snow to steam in his mind's eye.

"Hey, you're supposed to be smoothing the bumps, not erasing the wall," Eddie called, dropping the load of scraps into the large garbage can in the center of the room.

"What? Oh, sorry. Guess I don't know my own strength," Add managed to answer, his voice raspy to his ears. He had to get her out of there before he attacked her and carried her off to their room to ravage her body. "What's for supper?"

"I thought we'd do burgers on the grill," she answered easily, bending over for another load of scraps.

Add faced the wall and tried to draw air into his lungs. He

counted the breaths, waiting for a calm that wasn't coming. "Does Chloe like burgers?"

"No. Neither does Charles," Eddie answered, reaching for the broom. "But they'll be at a faculty dinner party. Which means we get to eat what we want."

Add moaned softly. He searched his mind for an innocuous topic of conversation. Anything that wouldn't remind him they'd be alone in the house—together. "What time's practice?"

"I canceled it. It's just too hot," Eddie said, bending to brush the small scraps into a dustpan just as Add peeked over his shoulder. Emptying it into the can, she leaned the broom against the wall and stretched, arms over her head, rotating her neck and twisting her back to relieve the kinks.

He felt the grit of the sandpaper bite into his hand as his fist tightened around it. Pain. That was good. Distracting. He concentrated on the pain.

"Well, I guess I'll get a shower before I start the grill," Eddie said and, with a breezy wave, left the room.

Add sagged against the wall and slid to the floor. He threw his head back, closed his eyes and dragged air into his starved lungs. He should have run hard and fast in the opposite direction as soon as he'd found her alone in this room. But no, not Add Rivers, good Samaritan, best buddy, all-around good guy.

"Rivers, you're a masochist," he muttered to himself, rising to face the wall, sandpaper at the ready. "Not only that, you're a fool, a lunatic. You are absolutely certifiable if you think for one minute you can continue sharing a room with that woman and just be friends."

He found a bump and sanded it. His strokes were short and jerky as he struggled to gain control of his body but the wall was smooth in seconds. He attacked another lump, and then another as he argued with himself.

While she saw him as a friend, he wanted to be her lover but it wouldn't be right, not now. Not before she had time to get over Charles. If Eddie ended up in his bed, it had to be because she wanted him as much as he wanted her, and that wasn't likely to happen in a matter of weeks.

In no time, every wall in the room was smooth, but he couldn't say the same for the road ahead of him. He could see only two options and neither made him happy. He could leave the house and end the constant contact with Eddie that was driving him crazy, but then she'd have to face Charles and Chloe alone. He could stay and back her up until the gruesome twosome finally departed and his sanity was a thing of the past.

"Who wants to be sane anyway?" he mumbled to himself, heaving the sandpaper into the garbage can. "It can't be all it's cracked up to be."

Eddie jerked open the door to the linen closet, yanked out two large bath towels and slammed the door. Mumbling and muttering to herself she stomped over to turn on the water in the tub. She stripped off her clothes, missing the clothes hamper by a mile before stepping into the shower.

Warm water sluiced over her body. With a curse, she spun the dials until needle-sharp pinpoints of spray pelted her with icy water. She hung her head beneath it and waited for her indignation to wash away. It didn't.

"Two weeks. Two weeks! He hasn't come within a mile of me in two weeks unless Charles and Chloe are standing in the room," she told the shower head. "I wear shorts so tight I can hardly breath after I snap myself in. I go without a bra, risking my boobs sagging to my navel before I hit thirty. Does he notice? No-o-o. He probably wouldn't notice me if I sat naked in his lap!"

She squeezed a big dollop of shampoo into her hand, and began massaging it into her hair. Her scalp tingled beneath the assault of her fingers.

She struggled for calm as she rinsed her hair. The water, parting around her breasts, coming together again to slip down her belly and legs, reminded her of the fantasy of Add making slow, delicious, fantastic love to her that haunted her every moment, awake or asleep. Her vigorous scrubbing made her skin tingle in exactly the same way it tingled whenever Add brushed against her or even just glanced at her.

She gave up trying to wash the thoughts away and climbed from the tub. Drying off, she glowered at the revealing clothes now lying in a heap beside the hamper. If the man had one ounce, one drop, of lust in his body for hers, those clothes should have ignited an inferno.

"It's hopeless," she muttered, wrapping the clothes in her towel and shoving them deep into the hamper.

She pulled on an over-sized cotton shirt over baggy shorts and headed downstairs. She'd promised hamburgers on the grill. The least she could do was feed the man, even if he didn't respond to her as other than a friend.

Add had more or less gained control of his libido an hour later when he joined Eddie in the backyard. Glass in one hand, he sauntered out the door, sniffing appreciatively the aroma of smoke, meat, and new-mown grass that filled the air. Thankfully, there wasn't the slightest hint of lilac to upset his hard-won restraint as long as he stayed downwind of Eddie.

"Medium or well-done?" she asked without turning to face him.

"Medium," he returned, eyeing her baggy clothes with a touch of disappointment. He felt his body tense in response to her nearness while his mind supplied a picture of what his eyes couldn't see.

Eddie slipped a broiled patty into a bun and passed the plate to Add, careful not to make contact with any part of him. Fixing one for herself, she took a seat on the bench beside the picnic table while Add claimed the opposite side.

They ate in silence, passing bowls of potato salad and cole slaw back and forth whenever they took some for themselves. Neither heard the crickets beginning their nightly serenade. The brilliant reds and pinks of the sunset went unnoticed as they kept their attention on the plates before them.

Unable to stand the silence a moment longer, Add said, "Getting Charles and Chloe to help with the renovation has been a bust."

"Yeah," Eddie agreed, screwing lids on each of the condiment jars slowly and carefully.

"Doesn't look like they'll run out of excuses not too help any time soon." Add collected the plates and silverware in front of him.

"Doesn't look like they're packing to leave either," Eddie answered with a sigh, clasping her hands on the table when everything was grouped to her satisfaction.

"Maybe the floor sander will do the trick," Add suggested, folding his arms on the table and looking off into the distance.

"Dynamite won't do the trick."

"You're probably right."

A strained silence began to grow between them.

"I saw Harriet Wolfe today," Eddie finally threw out.

"She ready to face the grind again?"

"No. She and Fred are planning to take the kids to the lake next week."

"That'll be nice for them."

"I know you don't like snakes," Eddie ventured, peeking from under her lashes at Add and then darting her glance away. "How do you feel about birds?"

"Huh?" Add said, finally looking at Eddie in confusion.

"Harriet took the birds from the science room home for the summer," Eddie explained, seemingly engrossed with twisting her fingers together. "She needs someone to take care of them while they're gone."

Add sat up straighter.

"She wants to know if I'll take care of them."

The left side of Add's mouth tipped upwards.

"Harriet said they're not much bother, unless you've got carpet, and we don't," she hurriedly added.

The right side of Add's mouth joined the left. "Are we

discussing those three foul-mouthed parrots Jefferson brought back to study? How did Harriet end up with them?''

''They're Pygmy parrots and Harriet was browbeaten into it,'' Eddie explained. ''She's working on improving their vocabulary.''

''The parsonage will probably never be the same. Reverend Wolfe must love it,'' Add said, a chuckle escaping to float away on the night breeze.

''Everyone thought they'd learn better behavior in the parsonage,'' Eddie said, defending the principal's choice for a summer home for the avian trio. ''Fred's been very understanding about the whole thing.''

''Have they learned anything?''

''No, but Harriet and the kids have,'' Eddie answered with a giggle.

''Oh, no.'' Add broke into a deep roar of laughter. When he finally conquered it, he dared to ask, ''Dare I ask why carpet would be a problem?''

''Well they stay on their perch most of the time.'' Eddie began trying to force her face into serious lines. ''But sometimes they fly around the house.''

Add waited, staring at Eddie, waiting for the other shoe to drop.

''They tend to scatter their food all over the floor under the perch,'' Eddie added.

''Uh-uh.''

''There is some feather loss from time to time.''

''Go on.''

''They fly just before they do their business,'' Eddie finished, grinning.

Add grinned back. ''By business you mean little white blobs in inconvenient places.''

Add bent double, laughing wildly as he pictured their housemates up against the terrible trio.

Eddie joined the merry sound with her own lighter, tinkling laughter. Each time she thought she'd gained control, she'd meet Add's eyes and break out in fresh peals. She hugged herself, trying to hold it back when her sides began to ache. The laughter turned to giggles, then chuckles, and she gasped for breath, ultimately gaining control. She refused to glance toward Add, afraid she'd start laughing again.

Add lay back across the picnic bench and stared at the stars as he struggled to contain himself and breath again. He took deep gulps of air and gradually calm descended. Without moving from where he lay, he asked, "You want us to take them?"

"It beats going with the ten foot snake," Eddie answered.

"I take it they haven't been taught to aim for specific targets?"

"Afraid not."

Eddie heard the quavery breath clearly in the dark and knew she'd won at least this battle.

"Hide the children. Bring on the flying storm troopers," Add told her, sitting up and grinning across the table. "Just make sure you keep *our* door shut."

Eddie held up three fingers in a scout pledge and grinned back.

"When are they arriving?" he asked, pushing up from the table and beginning to gather the remains of their supper in his arms.

"Next week. I'll pick them up on my way home from school," Eddie answered, copying Add before heading toward the house.

"Battle stations," Add called at the roar of a sports car in the drive. Catching the door with his foot, he followed Eddie inside.

Struggling through the back door, an overflowing bag of groceries in each arm and her book bag dangling from her shoulder, Eddie couldn't see what she'd bumped into.

"Edwina, look what your couch has done to my slacks," Charles complained loudly.

Eddie struggled to peek between the two bags. All she could see was his mottled red face. Taking a cautious step to the side, she skirted him and set the bags on the kitchen counter.

She glanced up and down his doubled-pleated trousers but couldn't see anything abnormal.

"They look fine to me."

Eddie took a head of lettuce and gallon jug of milk toward the refrigerator.

Charles turned his backside to Eddie. "They're ruined."

Eddie glanced down, noted the thread that had been pulled, and shrugged. "I can fix that with a crochet hook. I do it all the time. I think I've got one around here somewhere."

Charles grabbed her arm and spun her around. "This is all your fault. There's a bad spring in the couch. If you could have cushions made, why didn't you have it properly repaired?"

Eddie spoke calmly. "I made the cushions myself. The material cost $1.89 on the remnant table. Fixing the springs would have cost several hundred dollars."

Charles scowled.

"The spring doesn't pop between the cushions unless you sit in one particular place, so I just avoid that spot," Eddie said.

He continued to scowl at her but apparently could find no words to express his outrage in face of her calm.

"If you want, I'll fix the pants for you," she offered. "Did you need them right away?"

Throwing his hands in the air, Charles stormed from the kitchen. Whistling, Eddie turned back to the items still standing on the counter and began fixing a meatloaf for supper. She had it finished and in the oven within minutes.

She collected her purse and keys and headed for the door. Today was the day she got the birds from Harriet Wolfe.

Chapter 12

Add lay on the blow-up mattress and grinned into the darkness as an outraged screech split the night. He heard the muffled giggle even through the pillow and he could picture Eddie, in the bed above him, holding her fist against her mouth.

"Another direct hit," he whispered to the room at large and was pleased to hear Eddie's muffled giggle.

"That's three hundred and seventeen," she whispered. "Do you think I'm giving the birds too much food?"

"Chloe and Charles are still here, aren't they?"

"I'll double their sunflower seeds tomorrow. Have they caught you yet?"

"Not once in three days," Add answered softly. "Those birds are more discerning than I thought."

They lay in silence, listening to Charles's voice rumble over Chloe's near-hysterical French.

"How're the floors coming?" Add asked when the voices finally stilled.

"Almost ready for finishing," Eddie said, turning on her side to peek over the edge of the bed at Add on the floor. "Add, what does *ânesse* mean?"

"What?" he asked, pushing up onto his elbow and looking back at Eddie, her hair tousled and falling forward over the side of the bed.

"*Anesse.* When I turned the sander on about seven this morning Chloe started shouting it at ... well, I'm not sure if it was Charles or me," she said with a shrug of her shoulders.

The moonlight streaming into the window allowed Eddie to see Add's lips turn up in a smile.

"I think that's a part of the horse you don't want to discuss," he answered, reaching up to capture an errant curl and wrap it around his finger.

"I see," she replied a little breathlessly, her glance sweeping across Add's chest and the indentations of rippling muscle the moon allowed her to glimpse.

"Anyone asked about suitcases?"

"No, although Charles is making notes about the furniture again," Eddie said, dropping one arm over the side of the bed to tangle in his hair.

Add tugged on the curl and then let it slip slowly from his finger. "I noticed the books he brought home yesterday. None on economics but several on antiques."

"He's not getting my furniture," she said sternly, her hand balling into a fist in front of Add's nose.

Add raised his hands as if fending off an attack. "Hey, I'm innocent."

Eddie's first bumped ever so gently against Add's nose. "That's too bad," she whispered beneath her breath before withdrawing her hand and flopping back toward the center of the bed.

Familiar night sounds filled the room, carried on the breeze that gently lifted the sheers at the windows and cooled the room. Eddie concentrated on the rustling leaves and the distant sound of a car slipping through the night. She tried to pinpoint every single sound and catalogue it in her mind. It was a new cure for insomnia someone had been expounding on the radio that morning. As far as she was concerned, it didn't work.

A blood-curdling shriek brought Eddie bolt upright in bed. Add vaulted it and was halfway across the room when the door burst open, threatening to bring down the ceiling.

"Edwina, this will stop now!" Charles roared, shoving past Add and advancing on the bed.

"What?" she asked, dragging the sheet up to her chin and sliding toward the far side of the bed.

"You will have those flying fertilizer factories out of this house tomorrow." Charles grabbed her arms and shook her violently. He released her the moment he felt Add's hand clamp onto his shoulder.

"Back off," Add ordered, his voice low and fierce as he grabbed Charles by the shoulder and spun him around. "Don't you ever put a hand on my wife again or you'll answer to me."

"You don't fool me for a minute," Charles growled, knocking the hand from his shoulder. "I know what you're trying to pull here and it won't work. You and your little wife will not drive me from this house. If you persist in terrorizing Chloe with your little stunts, I'll see you in court for assault. By the time I'm finished, I'll have this house and everything in it plus whatever you might earn for the next 50 years!"

Add scowled at the shorter man, his brows lowered and eyes dark. He folded his arms across his chest, the muscles in his shoulders and arms bunching in readiness for action.

"Your name may be on the deed for this house for the time being, but Eddie's name is there, too. That means she has equal rights here. If she chooses to keep birds, she'll keep birds. If she chooses to keep snakes, I'll help her find one, although why she'd want to deal with another one, I don't know," Add ground out.

Grabbing Charles by the arm, he marched him to the door. "Unless you want us invading your privacy, you will learn to knock on this door if you have something to say to us." He pushed Charles out. "If I were you, I wouldn't make any more threats."

With that, Add slammed the door in Charles' face and turned

the key in the lock, nearly breaking it off with his forcefulness. He dropped his forehead against the door and took a slow, deep breath through his mouth. His fists braced against the door to either side of his head, their knuckles white in his fury.

A tiny sob behind him cleared the haze of fury from his mind. He consciously relaxed his hands, bringing them to his side before he turned to face Eddie.

She lay crumpled in a tight ball on the bed, her cries muffled by the sheet she'd jammed against her mouth. The sight tore at him, threatening to drive him down the hall to pound on the fool who'd caused her such grief. *That won't do her any good,* he told himself as he moved to the bed and sat down, drawing her onto his lap and cradling her head against his shoulder.

"Cry it out, honey," he said, smoothing tangled curls away from her face. "I won't let him hurt you."

He held her close while she cried, his hand gliding up and down her slender back, allowing himself to take pleasure in the feel of her soft breasts pressed against his chest. The ache that built low in his belly urged him to let the moment drag on, but he knew he shouldn't, and couldn't. With a groan, he relaxed his hold.

"It's not working," she mumbled, her words muffled against his chest.

"Sure it is. We just have to give it time," Add assured her, his hand gliding up and down her back.

"How much time can it take? They're no closer to leaving than they were the day they arrived," she stated flatly, her fingers stroking the muscles of his chest absently. "Maybe I should just let him have the house."

Add held her away from him and, when she wouldn't meet his eyes, he cupped her chin in his hand and lifted it until their eyes met. "But you love this house."

"Not enough to let Charles hurt you to get it."

"He won't hurt me," Add told her as new tears cascaded down her cheeks.

Eddie's arms tightened around him, clutching at the security he offered. She tried to stop the tears that splashed down her face and wet his chest. It didn't work. She buried her face in Add's comforting, warm, powerful chest.

Until he heard her hiccup and take a deep, shuddery breath, Add had no sense of place. He'd not considered that he sat in a skimpy pair of jogger's shorts holding a scantily-clad Eddie in his lap, her soft curves molded against him. Suddenly it occurred to him and immediately his body surged to life. He gritted his teeth, fighting to control the desire to draw her closer, to drive himself deep into her, to make them one.

Perhaps weeks of sharing a room with her, inhaling her scent with every breath he took, dreaming about the silky texture of her skin beneath his hands, had endowed him with superhuman strength. It wasn't easy to fight himself but he thought he was winning until she turned her tear-drenched eyes up to him.

Maybe it was the melting plea in those stormy green eyes, or her hand resting against his thundering heart. Maybe he was just too tired of the battle to resist any longer when her lips trembled and lifted to his.

With a groan of surrender, he released her to slip his fingers deep into her long, tangled mane and cradle her head as delicately as a new-picked rose. Searching her emerald eyes, he found no doubts, no hesitation. What he saw reflected in the clear depths was a yearning to match his own.

His hands trembled as he drew her closer, one thumb outlining her full bottom lip until it was the single thing separating them. When she quivered under his gentle touch, he could hold back no longer. His head bowed to meet hers until their lips could join, fuse, claim what he'd waited an eternity for.

He wanted to savor each moment, each second, as she not only surrendered to his kiss but answered it in full measure, but it was impossible. Knowing she wanted him as much as he desired her, broke down every barrier he'd kept between them for the past year. He held nothing back as he devoured her very essence, drinking in her sweet warmth like a drowning man seeking water.

Judith Hershner

He showered kisses across her cheeks to her eyes, her temples, her exquisitely shaped ears. He teased with his tongue, learning every twist and turn and secret crevice before slipping down the neck she angled to give him freer access. His hands slipped from her hair to glide over her back, drawing her closer to him, supporting her quivering frame.

Add barely skimmed the silky skin of her neck and shoulders, letting his lips and tongue savor it before moving on to taste the lilac-scented flesh that rose above the V neck of her sleep shirt and hinted at her full breasts still hidden from view.

Eddie could hardly breathe for the sensations that swamped her consciousness but she didn't care. She'd give up breathing in an instant to experience the flames Add's lips were trailing across her heated flesh. Her hands clenched in his hair, holding on for dear life to the one constant in the madness that his kisses created, holding him near, urging him on.

Soon, accepting his kisses wasn't enough. She needed to feed the fire that raged inside her. As he explored her neck, her shoulders, she probed the corded muscles of his, drawing her tongue along the rigid tendons and sinews. But she couldn't get enough. The lower his head dipped to taste her heated flesh, the less she had to savor.

When her mouth could go no further, she drew her hands from the springy depths of his hair to caress the strong back that trembled slightly at her gentle touch. Slowly at first, her fingers slid down his responsive spine. She'd fantasized many times about what it would be like to run her fingers over his back, have him above her, feel his flesh burn at her touch. The fantasy fell far short of reality.

Her fingers slipped beneath his jogger shorts and he bucked wildly at the touch. She slid her hands lower, reaching for, embracing, encompassing his tight male behind only to be stopped by the bed they still sat upon. She leaned into him, forcing her aching breasts against his rock-hard chest, trying to tumble him backwards but he couldn't be budged.

Changing course, he sought out and kissed the gentle slope that led to her full breasts.

A growl escaped from deep in his throat when she moved against him, pushing her breasts into his chest, tempting him unmercifully. He held himself rigid as he fought to hold himself in check, tried to ignore her hands on his buns, massaging, drawing him closer. It was too soon, much too soon. He didn't want to take her in a mad rush.

She shifted in his arms to trail up through the light furring of hair on his chest until she found his nipples and began teasing them. Her sighs of pleasure at their immediate response sapped his resolve, and he tumbled back onto the bed.

He lost all interest in restraint when she dipped her head and her lips, her tongue, and then her teeth, found the small nubbins buried in his mat of chest hair. His hands flew to the tail of the shirt that had bunched about her waist. Grabbing it, he jerked it up and off, and turned, trapping her beneath his weight. He cupped her full breasts in his hands, his thumbs circling the rosy aureolas, drawing closer to the peak before pulling back, teasing her as she had teased him.

His hands felt so good on her, as they gently kneaded her breasts. He pressed them together before he dipped his head and rubbed his beard-roughened cheeks between them. She arched her back, offering herself for his pleasure, burning to have his mouth claim what she offered. She held her breath as his thumbs taunted her erect nipples, waiting, hoping, ready to plead with him if he didn't release her from the agony of waiting soon.

Eddie whimpered when he finally allowed the tip of his tongue to touch her nipple, first one and then the other.

She couldn't be still, couldn't stand his slow exploration. She wanted him, all of him, now. She could feel his arousal hard against her thigh, but he held himself just beyond the aching part of her that strained to meet him.

In a frenzy to appease the clamoring demands of her body, she dropped her hands to his back, urging him nearer but he refused to budge. Her hands glided lower until they encountered the shorts he still wore. Scratching him in her eagerness, she shoved the shorts down to the length of her reach.

She felt his flesh quiver in response to the contact. She eased her leg down the length of his again, then dragged it back up, savoring the moans of pleasure that escaped him at the contact.

Add released her breasts and threw his head back, gritting his teeth at the pleasure-pain that threatened to push him over the edge each time she moved. He tried to blank out the hunger to be inside her. It was a wasted effort. He couldn't quench the fierce desire that raged in his groin.

When she eased his shorts lower, and he felt the soft cloth move slowly over the supersensitized flesh of his aroused manhood, he knew he would explode. Unable to stand it, he dropped his hand to finish the job himself.

Her delicate fingers captured his before he could reach his objective and pressed them to her belly, dragging them across the velvety surface, guiding them lower with each sweep.

She urged the tip of his finger into the petals that hid her moist center, and bucked against him at the first contact of his rough hand with her silky core. He brought his damp finger back and circled it around the sensitive nub again and again, pleasuring her and taking pleasure in her wild response.

He barely heard her calling his name, pleading with him to hurry as he teased and tantalized, giving her small glimpses of the ecstasy that awaited her before drawing back to begin the process all over again.

Eddie was almost out of her mind with the sensations that flooded her being. She ached with longing. She stretched, trying to reach him, to capture him as he had captured her.

She guided him forward, rubbing the tip of him against her moist core until she felt like she held the heat of the sun within her hand. He bucked and strained against her now, as eager as she to complete what they'd started. With the slightest lift of her hips, she teased him, allowing him entrance, but just entrance, before she drew back.

Add could take no more. He captured Eddie's hands, pulling them high above her head, and anchored them there while his lips claimed hers. His tongue thrust deep into her mouth at the same time he pressed forward, burying himself deep inside her until he could feel her heart racing in time with his own.

Surrendering his control at last, he drove back into her again and again.

They met and plunged toward heaven and beyond, soaring into paradise and the sweet oblivion of lovers' sleep.

Nestled in Add's arms, Eddie smiled in her sleep and relived her wildest fantasies, knowing they were fantasies no more.

The woman of his dreams secure in his arms, Add no longer tossed and turned, but surrounded her gently with his strong arms and wished for nothing more.

Eddie, dressed in a paint-smeared T-shirt and speckled cut-offs, swore softly when the doorbell peeled. Pushing the floor tarp more securely beneath her arm, she grumbled and turned away from the stairs toward the front door. Shifting the brushes to the hand with the paint can, she opened it.

"May I help you?" she asked of the impeccably dressed stranger before her.

"I'm Al Crocker of Holmes Realty," he said, thrusting his hand forward and pumping Eddie's vigorously. "Was it you I spoke to on the phone about a week ago?"

"Uum, yes, I think it was," Eddie replied, pulling her hand back and flexing her fingers. "Did you have an appointment with Mr. Whitney?"

"No. Oh, no. I just happened to be in the neighborhood." He smiled broadly as he took a step into the house.

Eddie stepped back, not anxious to admit the man, but unable to stop him with her arms full of paint supplies. For a fleeting moment she wondered if a paint can dropped from a height of four feet could break a toe, but discarded the thought. She didn't want anything to delay Mr. Crocker.

"Is there something I can do for you?" she asked, displeased at the way he was craning his neck to inspect the inside of the house.

"I just wanted to drop some papers by for Mr. Whitney. Would he happen to be at home?"

"I'm afraid not. He has a meeting at the University," Eddie explained, stepping in front of Mr. Crocker and trying to herd him toward the door. "I'll tell him you called when he gets back."

"No need. No need at all. I can just leave the papers with you," he said with a toothy grin as he lifted his briefcase and set it on the secretary. He popped the clasps open, unmindful of the way the hinges scraped across the delicate surface.

Eddie ground her teeth and waited while he searched the folders inside the case.

He handed several papers to Eddie. She managed to grasp them and slide the tarp back under her arm at the same time, forcing herself to smile.

"I'll be sure Mr. Whitney gets these the moment he gets home," she assured him, urging him toward the door with her paint can.

"I appreciate that. Really appreciate it," he told her, casting one more pleased glance about the tidy living room. "Have a nice day and remember Holmes Realty if you're in the market for a home."

Eddie managed to hold her smile in place until the door shut on the realtor, and she could look at the papers in peace. She froze in place when the signatures at the bottom caught her attention. The tarp slipped and plopped onto the floor unnoticed as she read them more closely.

She studied every word, and finally concentrated on one particular signature. No doubt about it. The name, signed with a flourish, was Edwina Mason.

Eddie's fingers tightened on the paper, her nails threatening to perforate the four pages completely. The name on the document agreeing to sell her house was hers, but there was no way the signature came close to matching her own neat copper-plate handwriting.

She had him now. The little weasel had out-weaseled himself. She wasn't going to wait any longer. He'd be gone the moment she could get her hands on a phone book and the name of a lawyer.

"Hey, Coach, you in here?" a voice called from the kitchen. Other voices joined in. Her team. They were here. What were they doing here?

"I'm in the living room," she called out, hastily folding the paper with one hand and shoving it into her pocket.

Eleven girls tumbled through the kitchen door. All were dressed in scruffy, patched shorts and grungy T-shirts, and each one carried a paintbrush in her hand.

"Heard you were painting today."

"We wanted to help."

"Faster we get done, the sooner we can party."

Eddie's smile was a little woebegone but she managed one for her eager volunteers. "You don't have to help."

"We know that, Coach, but you've been really good to us."

"It's not like you had to be our Coach."

"Without you we wouldn't have a team."

"We wanted to say thanks."

"For the slumber party, too."

Eddie's smile became easier as her students crowded around her, their eager faces beaming at her.

"Thank you," she said graciously, passing the paint can and brushes to them and collecting the tarp from the floor. "If you're serious . . ."

"Of course, we're serious. You don't think we dress like this every day, do you?" someone in the back of the group called.

They all laughed and followed Eddie up the stairs.

Despite the teasing and gossip that could be expected whenever a group of teen-age girls got together, the painting went quickly. Eddie had just laid her brush aside to get some sodas and chips from the kitchen when Chloe appeared in the doorway.

Dressed to the nines in a sophisticated silk dress, she clutched the sides of the full skirt close to her body.

"What is causing this *terrible* smell?" she demanded, stepping back when one of the girls, paintbrush in hand, moved toward her.

"Hey, look at that dress!" the teen cried, drawing the attention of every other girl in the room.

"Is that a designer original?" another shouted over the oohs and aahs of the others.

Chloe ignored them, turning her angry gaze on Eddie. "How long will this stench last?"

Eddie stepped protectively in front of the girls. "Several days. I don't know exactly. As soon as the paint starts to dry we can turn on some fans and try to blow it out."

Chloe inspected the room without entering. "The color. Don't you find it a bit . . ." She waved at the pastel green walls. *"Provincial."*

"I find it restful. The lighter tones make the room seem so much larger and cheerier," Eddie answered, waving her own hand in imitation.

Before Chloe could respond, someone from the pack called out, "You want to help? We've got plenty of paintbrushes."

"She can't paint in that," someone else answered before Chloe could answer.

"She could borrow some of Coach's stuff," another voice suggested.

"That's quite out of the question," Chloe answered, her chill tones silencing the teens at last. She glared at Eddie a moment before finishing. "Charles and I are attending a faculty dinner this evening. One would hope that something can be done before we get back."

"One can always hope," Eddie agreed with a saccharine smile that didn't reach her eyes.

"Humph." Chloe turned on her heel, back rigidly straight, shoulders back, head high and left, to the relief of everyone.

Chapter 13

Add sat in the stands with the parents of the Hendricksburg team. His elbows rested on his thighs, his hands clasped between his knees as he watched Eddie talk to one of her team in the warm-up box. Checking the score board and then his watch, he glanced back to see Eddie sit down in the dugout.

He concentrated on the girl stepping up to the batter's box. If she could just hit a double, the runners waiting on first and second would make it home and the team would be conference champs. If she struck out, the season would end right here. He took a deep breath and held it as she took a practice swing before lifting the bat high over her shoulder.

By the time the count was two and three, Add was standing in the bleachers like every other Hendricksburg citizen, screaming his lungs out. As the pitcher wound up, he closed his eyes. He couldn't bear to see the poor kid strike out. The solid thunk of ball connecting with bat popped them open quickly.

The entire town seemed to be cheering as the ball sailed high over the field heading for deep right field. Add watched the outfielders race toward the ball, then stand uncertainly for a moment when it dropped between them. The center fielder grabbed the ball and threw toward second only to see Hendricksburg's batter rounding that base and heading for third.

Pandemonium broke out as the second baseman caught it, but overthrew third. Add was shaking hands and slapping the backs of everyone around him in the stands as the final runner slid into home. He surged forward toward the field with the rest of the Hendricksburg fans, his eager eyes seeking the long braid of auburn hair poked through the back of a baseball cap.

He finally found her at the center of a screaming, bouncing, jubilant group of teen-age girls who were in turn surrounded by parents and friends. Realizing the futility of making his way through the mass of bodies to her side, he began collecting the bats, balls, and stray equipment scattered about the dugout. The sooner he got them loaded into the van, the sooner they could head for home.

It was a good half-hour before the throng disbanded. Add reached Eddie's side. He threw an arm about her shoulders, kissed her on the cheek, and was rewarded with a thousand-watt smile.

"Did you see that hit?" Eddie crowed, hugging him about the waist. "The Babe himself couldn't have placed that ball better."

"World Series quality," Add agreed with her, raising his voice to be heard above the excited chatter of the girls who were finally beginning to gather gloves and water bottles together. "Probably the first woman in the majors."

Swatting good-naturedly at him, she directed one girl toward the lone baseball cap laying on the pitcher's mound and acknowledged a parent's thanks with a soft smile and nod of her head.

" 'Bout ready to head for home?" he asked, lowering his head to whisper in her ear.

Eddie rested her head on his chest for a moment as her adrenaline high began to ebb. "I've got to collect everything first," she explained with a weary sigh before stepping out of his embrace.

"Already done," he told her, catching her hand in his and lacing their fingers together.

"Bases?" she asked.

"Stored in the grounds shed," he returned, dangling the key chain he held before her.

"Then I guess I'm ready to go home." She took the key and pushed it deep into her jeans pocket as she fell into step beside him.

They listened to the dwindling voices as they ambled toward the parking lot. Fireflies blinked in the velvety night like miniature fireworks. The scent of charcoal fires filled the air, reminding them they'd skipped supper. Somewhere in the distance they heard a mother call her child home. Add's hand tightened about hers as they crossed the knoll where they'd come the night Eddie had begun to fight Charles.

Releasing her hand, Add pulled her securely against his side and dipped his head beneath the bill of her baseball cap to capture her lips in a short kiss.

"Mmm," Eddie murmured with a sigh as he pulled away.

"There could be more," he teased, urging her toward his waiting van.

"Are you suggesting we park somewhere and neck?" she asked, slipping from his arms.

"Not when there's a nice, soft, flat bed available."

"But there isn't. Did you forget the team celebration?" She came to an abrupt halt when he backed her into the side of the van, a hand on either side of her head.

He groaned and banged his head against the van. "How could I possibly forget a roomful of giggling teen-agers chasing me out of my bed? Are you sure I have to sleep in the den?"

Eddie turned her head to meet his hang-dog expression. A chuckle escaped before she ducked under his arm and opened the van door. Add's hand on her rounded bottom hurried her into the seat.

Stealing one more slow, lingering kiss, he drew back and shut the door before hurrying around the front of the van to join her. The engine roared to life and they headed out of the park toward home.

"Are you sure about this? I mean really sure?" Add asked.

"A promise is a promise," she answered, patting his arm and pointing down the street toward her house. "Besides, it looks like we're expected."

Add followed her gaze toward the cluster of teens waiting in the front yard of the old Victorian house. It didn't look like they'd waited for the hostess to arrive to begin partying. The radio of one of the cars parked at the curb was blaring rock and roll music into the night air. Teens danced and gyrated across the grass to the heavy beat of the music.

"Ah, well. Another time, another place," he said with an exaggerated sigh as he pulled into the driveway and turned off the van.

Before Eddie could grasp the handle of her door, it was pulled open and eager hands reached in to pull her out. Her laughter couldn't be heard over the raucous cheers of the teens who surrounded her. When strong arms lifted her into the air, she clutched frantically for hand holds. Wobbling precariously on the shoulders of her students, she was carried in triumph across the yard to the front door that Add held wide for the happy group.

Soda cans, empty chip bags, and remnants of hot dog buns littered every available inch of kitchen counter and table three hours later. Plastic garbage bag in hand, Add began systematically tossing the refuse into it. He didn't turn around when he heard the door open and a blast of rock music, girlish giggles, and lower-pitched laughter erupt into the room. He just reached for the next pile of paper plates.

"Good party?" Eddie asked, her tone weary as she sagged against the kitchen door.

"The most stupendous party ever according to the Rivers Party Rating System." Dropping the bag to the floor, he grasped Eddie's shoulders firmly and steered her toward one of the ladderback chairs at the table. It wasn't necessary to use force to get her to take the seat.

She closed her eyes as his strong fingers began massaging the knotted muscles in her neck and shoulders. Her head fell forward at the tender persuasion of his expert touch until she thought she might slip from the chair into a spineless puddle.

His warm breath at her neck set off tremors throughout her body. When his lips followed, she knew an earthquake fault line had been discovered at just that moment and the epicenter was her kitchen.

As the school clock on the wall chimed eleven o'clock, Eddie sighed and straightened her shoulders. "Time to send the boys home," she mumbled as she pushed to her feet and stumbled toward the dining room door.

"Need any help?" Add offered before picking up his trash bag.

Eddie leaned her shoulder against the door and took a deep breath. "No. At the moment they're all starting to droop. They'll moan and groan, but I think they'll head out quick enough."

Another hour saw the boys gone, the girls spread out in the guest room and the kitchen almost back to normal. Eddie enjoyed the peace that filled her home after the deafening racket earlier in the evening. It took a moment for her to realize that the giggles normal to twelve teens at a slumber party were conspicuously absent. She nudged Add who sat next to her, his eyes closed, his breathing growing slower now that the monumental clean-up was completed.

"Do you hear anything?" she asked when he lifted one eyelid and peered at her.

"Not a thing. Isn't it wonderful?" he answered, closing his eye again.

"No, it isn't wonderful," Eddie returned, sliding her chair back from the table.

"Doesn't silence mean they're finally asleep?" he mumbled without moving a muscle.

"Doubtful. It's only midnight." Eddie pushed to her feet and headed for the dining room door. "Quiet among teen-agers is a sure sign of trouble."

"Think they sneaked out to talk to the boys?" he asked, sliding his chair from the table but not rising. "Want me to come with you?"

"No, it's not the boys. Then we'd hear noise, not loud, but noise," Eddie said. "Maybe I'm wrong and all the exercise and excitement have put them all to sleep. I'll just go upstairs and check."

"Call if you need help," Add called after her retreating figure and relaxed back into his seat.

Eddie pulled herself up the stairs. Every step she asked herself why she'd proposed a slumber party for her baseball team to celebrate the end of the season. Rubbing her temples and yawning, she followed the few muffled sounds that now reached her.

Eddie froze when she found herself in the doorway of Chloe's bedroom. Her eyes widened in shock as she watched her baseball team pull gowns at random from the rack for inspection. Their sighing, oohing, and aahing echoed in her ears as she imagined what would happen if Chloe caught them running their hands over the delicate fabrics or fingering the intricate beadwork.

"Girls, what are you doing in here?" she asked softly from the door.

Twelve pairs of eyes darted to her face and guilty flushes crept up their cheeks.

"We only meant to see what was in here, honest, Coach."

"Isn't this the hottest dress you've ever seen?"

"Wow, Coach, why don't you wear any of these?"

"She must really be a model."

"Are these designer originals?"

"I'll bet they're expensive."

"Can't you see me in this at the prom?"

''Tommy Brown's eyes would pop out of his head if he saw me in this.''

Questions and comments bombarded her like a tidal wave. She tried separating them to make comments but her brain was already on overload. Moving to the nearest girl, she took the dress from her and placed it carefully back on the rack.

''These are Mrs. Whitney's things,'' she explained, heading for the next girl. ''Yes, they are very expensive and easily damaged. Mrs. Whitney wore most of these when she was a model in Paris. Please put everything back carefully right now. You all know better than to invade someone else's privacy this way.''

The girls moaned in disappointment but returned everything with lingering glances and heartfelt sighs. Their conversation was subdued as they gathered at the door to leave.

''Get out!'' Chloe screamed from the top of the stairs, dashing forward and grabbing the arm of the girl nearest her and pulling her from the room.

''How dare you defile my things. Get out! Get out!'' Crimson-faced with fury, she lapsed into rapid-fire French as she forced her way into the midst of the girls and began shoving them out of the room.

Catching sight of Eddie, she descended on her, bringing her hand down across Eddie's cheek.

Eddie's hand flew to her cheek but she said nothing. She felt the outrage of the girls who stood at her back and put out a hand to stop their instinctive rush to defend her.

''Hey, we didn't mean any harm.''

''Nothing got hurt.''

''We didn't spread any dirt, if that's what you're worried about.''

''Coach didn't have nothing to do with this.''

''Who'd want your old junk, anyway?''

''Hey, look, we're sorry.''

Chloe ignored the girls' words, their rushed apologies. Pushing them out of the room, she began dashing from rack to rack, inspecting each garment for damage.

"Sorry, Coach."

"We didn't mean for you to get in trouble."

"Yeah, we're really sorry."

The girls filed past Eddie to the guest room across the hall, pausing to look back at her before they hung their heads and entered. Eddie tried to offer a forgiving smile before motioning them to shut the door.

Add, awakened by the raised voices from his doze at the kitchen table, pushed past Charles at the top of the stairs to reach Eddie's side. Gently he ran a finger across the scarlet handprint on her cheek. His expression was furious. When he turned toward the closet room, Eddie laid a restraining hand on his arm.

She wanted to step into his reassuring arms and just lay her head on his chest. It would be so easy to let him handle the situation the way his expression said he wanted to but she couldn't let him do that. This was her battle, one she should never have involved him in. Lifting her chin defiantly, she stepped around him and entered Chloe's domain.

With single-minded intent, she marched up to the other woman, grabbed Chloe's arm as she'd seen her do minutes earlier to the girls, and spun her around.

"Don't you *ever* put your hands on my girls again," she hissed, her index finger thumping the model's flat chest and driving her back against her clothes.

"Then keep your precious girls away from my things," Chloe fired back, lifting one hand as if to slap Eddie again.

"I wouldn't do that if I were you," Eddie warned, catching the thin wrist in her hand. Her fingers tightened when Chloe tried to jerk it free.

Eddie heard a scuffle in the hall but ignored it, centering her attention on the woman before her.

"My girls were curious, so they looked. That's not a capital offense. They thought you were beautiful. They wanted to be like you. Thank God they never will. They've got hearts,'' Eddie said with a calm she didn't feel. ''No matter what their faces look like, no matter how old they are, the beauty down deep in those hearts will always shine while you fade away to nothing.''

Eddie released Chloe's wrist, turned and marched from the room. She nodded toward Add, who stood in the hall restraining an outraged Charles.

Eddie finally managed to calm the teens, and left them to talk silently among themselves until they dropped off to sleep.

The clock on her bedside table blinked two-thirty at her in bright red letters. With a groan, she dropped, exhausted, onto the bed that seemed overly large without Add's presence. She pulled his pillow into her arms and buried her nose in it, inhaling his familiar scent.

She lay sleepless, thinking. She'd intended the party as a reward for the girls' hard work during the summer. It hadn't turned out that way. Instead, they'd been forced to face the ugliness that sometimes lurked behind a beautiful face.

Eddie tossed and turned, twisting the sheets about her. It didn't help that Add was spending the night in a sleeping bag in her den. They'd agreed it wouldn't set a good example for the girls if he shared her room but she missed his presence. She'd have given almost anything to curl into his sheltering embrace.

She flopped to her side and pulled his pillow close. She closed her eyes and pretended he was there with her. Gradually her breathing slowed, the scent on his pillow creating the illusion of his presence. Eventually she slept.

The girls lay silently in their sleeping bags, concentrating fiercely on the sounds coming from the back bedroom. When the last door closed and no footsteps could be heard, they stealthily opened the door to the hall. Nodding toward one of their members, they waited while she crept across the hall and lay her ear against the door to the bedroom that still harbored voices.

Her brows drew down in a frown as she listened. It was only a matter of minutes before she slipped back into the guest room and silently closed the door behind her. The girls returned to their sleeping bags, stretching out once again they waited for her report.

"Well? What's going on?" the oldest girl demanded in hushed tones.

"What were they arguing about?"

"I don't know. They were talking French and it was too fast for me," the scout told them.

"Couldn't you understand anything?"

"A word here and there, but they didn't make any sense and I'm not sure I heard them right."

"I thought you got an A in French."

"I did, but our French teacher talks a lot slower. I can't believe they actually understand each other."

"Did you hear Coach's name?"

"Once or twice."

"The voices, how did they sound? Were they still mad?"

"Yeah, kind of."

"But?"

"Well, the guy sounded like my little brother when he's planning a prank that's gonna make me real mad."

"What about the slink?"

"The slink sounded kinda oily and real pleased with herself."

"You don't think they know about Coach, do you?"

"How could they?"

"Mr. Add is sleeping downstairs. Wouldn't that make them suspicious?"

"Why should it?"

"Well . . . you know."

"Don't you think Coach and Mr. Add look great together?"

"He is so dreamy."

"He can sweep me away any time."

''Do you think Coach loves him?''

''Yeah!''

''Think they'll get married when Charles and the slink are gone?''

''Sure, the hero always marries the girl.''

''This isn't one of your mom's books.''

''I know that but it's almost the same.''

''Think Coach will invite us to the wedding?''

One by one the girls' voices dwindled away as exhaustion overcame them and sleep claimed them.

No one noticed the soft click as their door was shut, but they hadn't noticed it open earlier either.

Chloe slipped back across the hall to the room she shared with Charles, a feral gleam in her eye. How appropriate that the little dears should know so much about their precious Coach. And how fortunate she had been there to overhear every word.

Chapter 14

The next morning, Eddie felt like left-over hash. The girls' first stirrings at 6:30 had awakened her. Bleary-eyed from too little sleep, she'd rolled out of bed, peeled off the jeans and team shirt she'd fallen asleep in and managed a quick shower before her team found the energy to seek out food.

Only half awake, even after a bracing shower, she'd emptied the pockets of yesterday's jeans and shoved the contents into her cut-offs. She noted in passing the letter of commitment she'd meant to talk to Add about. But she had twelve hungry teen-agers in her kitchen waiting for food.

She fixed a massive breakfast while the girls chattered away about their plans for the day. They didn't seem in the least subdued after their experience with Chloe the night before, although they conveyed a message of sorts about their feelings for her.

Pancakes, waffles, scrambled eggs, toast, sausage, bacon, and toast had vanished almost in the twinkling of an eye. Eddie and Add, who'd joined the group looking endearing with his stubbled cheeks and tousled hair, had breakfasted on the only food left by the hungry horde—French toast.

The bright smile on Eddie's lips as she stood on the porch to wave the girls off wasn't as forced as she'd expected it to be. She waited until the last car carrying the last team member turned off her street before squaring her shoulders and turning back to the house.

She needed to discuss this new development with Add, and followed the sound of his off key whistling back to the kitchen. She found a natural smile teasing the corners of her mouth as she pushed the door open.

"Must you whistle in the kitchen?" she pretended to complain, coming through the door.

Add finished stacking plates in the dishwasher before turning to answer her. "Why shouldn't I?"

"It's bad luck," Eddie explained, collecting the dirty glasses the girls had left around the room. "We don't need any more bad luck. Besides, there's something I need to tell you."

Taking the glasses and lining them up in the dishwasher, Add shut the door and flipped the switch to on. Still whistling his off-key rendition of a sixties song, he grabbed Eddie about the waist and began dancing her around the kitchen.

"No time for talk," he declared, picking up the rhythm. "Just dance."

"Stop it," Eddie grumbled, trying to hold in a laugh while clinging to Add for balance. "I'm trying to be serious."

"I am serious—about dancing," he answered, swinging her round in circles until she grew dizzy and flung her arms about his neck to remain upright.

Even when he stopped spinning and had to lean against the basement door for balance, he didn't release her. He watched her eyes darken to deepest green before lowering his head and capturing her lips. His tongue teased the soft curves of her mouth as fire blazed unchecked between them. Her answering sigh of pleasure as she opened her lips to him only added fuel to the fire.

He released her hands to hug her to him, matching her peaks to his valleys. He rubbed against her, letting her know the extent of the desire she kindled with her nearness. The need to be with her, feel himself in her, raged within him. He began guiding her toward the door to the dining room and the stairs beyond without abandoning her lips for a second.

Brring. Brring. The steady repetitive sound annoyed him as he pushed at the door with his shoulder. Eddie's hands tugging his shirt from his form-hugging jeans made it easy to ignore the sound.

Brring. Brring. He lifted his head only long enough to glare at the phone before kissing her face and proceeding to nibble his way down her neck toward the inviting cleft between her soft breasts.

Brring. Brring. The sound grew muffled as the door shut behind them and Add lifted Eddie into his arms. He moved purposefully through the rooms toward the stairs.

"Isn't someone going to get that infernal telephone?" Charles shouted down the stairs.

The phone, and more importantly, their noisy house guest, could be ignored no longer.

Add's arms tightened about Eddie as he buried his head in her neck while they both struggled for breath.

Brring. Brring.

"Well?"

Add threw his head back and took a final breath to clear the desire from his mind. "I'll get it," he said finally. His voice was impatient.

They heard the bedroom door above them shut as the phone rang again. Add set Eddie on her feet, a look of utter frustration on his face as he met her passion-dark eyes. As the phone rang again, he placed a gentle kiss on her lips before stepping away and hurrying toward the kitchen.

Eddie sagged against the wall, mumbling curses on the fool who'd invented the telephone. She smoothed her T-shirt down across her breasts. They were heavy with the need to feel Add's hands upon them. When the fabric rubbed across her sensitive nipples, she almost moaned.

The sound of the kitchen door opening threatened to shatter the little composure she'd regained. When she saw how downcast Add's face was, the struggle grew easier.

Wrapping her in his arms, Add pulled her close and nestled his cheek against her hair. "Alexander Bell should be glad he's dead," he grumbled near her ear. "I've been having some very violent ideas concerning him the last few minutes."

"Worse then making him listen to Metallica tapes for hours?" Eddie asked, melting into his embrace.

"Oh, definitely worse," he replied, his voice raspy as his hands slid down her back and settled on her waist. With a light kiss against her temple, he pulled away and met her questioning glance. "Sam Dortman just tripped over a poodle and broke his leg."

"That's too bad," she said, her brows lowered in confusion. "But what . . ."

"Someone is going to have to finish his route," Add explained, his hands tightening about her waist to draw her to him for a brief, intense kiss. "Carl's out of town on vacation, and guess who's left?"

"But this is your day off," Eddie protested, her own hands slipping into his still open shirt to trace his ribs.

Sparks darted along every nerve ending in his body. "You wouldn't really leave me alone with them?" she asked, interspersing her words with kisses along his sternum and the firm muscles on either side.

"It's not my first choice," Add managed to gasp as Eddie's lips slipped lower. He had to force his mind to concentrate on the words while her hands explored his torso. "But neither snow nor rain . . ."

"We're in the middle of a drought," she informed him, her lips nearing his waistband.

"Nor heat or gloom of night," he pointed out, his eyes closed, his head thrown back with pleasure.

"That's the sun out there," she said, her fingers insinuating themselves between his flat stomach and the waistband of his snug jeans.

"Stays these couriers," he said, his voice gruff as his fingers clutched her shoulders and lifted her up. "From the swift completion of their appointed rounds."

"What about a hot woman?" she whispered, laying her head against his chest and slipping her tongue from between her lips to tease his flat nipple.

If it hadn't been for the door slamming upstairs, Add might have succumbed to the blatant invitation. With a deep-throated growl he caught her wandering hands in his and stepped back. "Later," he rasped, kissing her fiercely before hurrying up the stairs.

When he came back, uniformed, Eddie was draped along the newel post, her hands clasped behind her back stretching her T-shirt temptingly across her full breasts. Add moaned at the sight and allowed himself only a quick, hot meeting of their lips before forcing himself out the door.

Alone and frustrated, Eddie was no longer the least bit sleepy. *Activity,* she told herself firmly. *You need physical activity.* It was a sure bet she wouldn't be able to concentrate on anything until the energy that should have gone to more pleasurable occupations was dissipated.

Grabbing her purse, Eddie headed out the door. She wasn't about to spend the morning alone in her house with Chloe and Charles. Just the thought of those two scheming vipers would be enough to chase away the wonderful feeling of anticipation that bubbled through her.

A morning of yard-sale hopping dissipated Eddie's need for activity with a vengeance. She felt like a wet mop by the time she returned to the house just after noon, but the pleasurable glow of anticipating Add's touch was still with her. On the way home she'd decided an afternoon nap would revive her sufficiently for her evening with Add.

Her lips were tilted up in a secret smile when she pushed

the front door open. The smile vanished the moment she saw Charles and a stranger examining her dining room table.

"Who's this, Charles?" she demanded as she joined them in the dining room.

"Edwina, this is Harold Masters," Charles explained in an unctuous tone. "He owns Masters' Antiques. Mr. Masters, this is Edwina Mason."

"Miss Mason. I'm so pleased to meet you," the small, elderly man with the balding head said, as he offered his hand. "You've done an excellent job restoring this piece. You know, so many people destroy the finer details of the claw feet," he went on enthusiastically without giving her a moment to interrupt. "And I noticed how careful you were to retain the craftsman's mark. Excellent workmanship. Excellent."

Before she could thank him for the compliment, he'd turned back to the table and was running his hand lovingly along the top.

"Charles, perhaps we should talk in the kitchen," Eddie forced out between lips stiff with suppressed anger.

"After Mr. Masters has gone," he returned, shrugging her hand from his sleeve.

Mr. Masters rounded the corner of the table and turned his attention to the china cabinet against the far wall. "But I'm so glad you contacted me when you decided to sell your antiques. Such pieces are rarely in good condition. I know of several buyers who'd be willing to pay handsomely to own these."

"Pardon me?" Eddie said, ignoring Charles' frown. Dark red tinted her cheeks as she tried to restrain her anger. It wouldn't be right to take out the fury and resentment that bubbled inside her on the antique dealer. "Have you been led to believe I wish to sell my table?"

"Why, yes, my dear. Although I don't understand why you would want to part with such pieces after all the work of restoring them." He cast a last loving look for the china cabinet before turning to face Eddie.

"I'm afraid there's been a misunderstanding," she said gently, taking his arm and directing him toward the front door. "I'm not interested in selling any of my furniture."

"But Mr. Whitney was quite clear on the telephone," Mr. Masters objected, looking back toward Charles who shrugged his shoulders.

"He was?" Eddie asked, slowing her forward motion and meeting Mr. Masters eye to eye. "What exactly did Mr. Whitney say?"

"He explained that you had acquired all of these lovely items while you had been engaged." The little man coughed delicately into his hand while a flush crept up his cheeks. "Since you had broken off the engagement, he said you wanted to sell the furniture in order to make a fresh start without old memories to haunt you."

"How thoughtful of Mr. Whitney," she said, forcing a smile for the elderly gentleman. "The truth is that I've grown very attached to my furniture. More attached to it, in fact, than Mr. Whitney and I were to each other. I don't think we'll be requiring your services at this time."

"Oh dear. I've already spoken to my best customers about your pieces," Mr. Masters protested, albeit mildly.

"Perhaps after Mr. Whitney and I have settled things between ourselves, we'll give you a call," Eddie said to soothe the man's obviously agitated state. She led him toward the door.

With a final, longing look toward the furniture, he extended his hand to Eddie and nodded to Charles. "Yes, perhaps that's best. It's always painful to part with the things that remind us of better times."

"Exactly," Eddie said, opening the door and ushering the man out before her fixed smile could slip.

The latch had barely snapped into place when Eddie rounded on Charles. Her back was ramrod straight as she stalked him, her glance steely hard as it bored into his, making him back away before her determined strides.

"Now, Edwina," Charles tried, his tone placating. "I've

talked to a number of people recently and I've been running the numbers.''

"Oh, have you really?" she ground out, stopping just out of his reach.

"The amount of appreciation on the house since the repairs is astronomical," he said, enthusiasm entering his voice. "After the mortgage is satisfied at the bank, we'll earn over $24,000 apiece. Combine that with the value of the furniture, and the total comes to nearly $45,000 for each of us."

Eddie stared at him, her hands fisted on her hips. "Forty-five thousand dollars?" she asked evenly. "Is that all profit?"

"Yes, and if we sink it into another property within six months, it isn't taxable, either," Charles explained with a smile and a bright gleam in his eye. "That's almost $3,800.00 a month for very little effort."

Eddie dropped her hands to her sides and advanced on Charles. "Thirty-eight hundred for very little effort, you say?"

"I've got the figures if you want to see them," he assured her, folding his arms across his puffed-up chest.

"I don't need to see your figures," she informed him, her index finger prodding his soft belly. "I earned that money. All of it. The hard way."

Charles left eye narrowed as she began pacing the room.

"How much is Mr. Masters willing to pay for the table?" she asked softly, running her hand along its gleaming top.

"He's offered five thousand but I'm sure we can get another thousand out of him. I've been checking out some antique books and tables of this caliber that are selling to collectors for eight to ten thousand. Not a bad profit for a twenty-dollar outlay."

"Four thousand percent profit might be considered good," Eddie admitted, taking a second to straighten the lace doily and the floral center piece in the middle of the table. "Not bad at all if *we* bought the table as it stands today for twenty dollars. Did you give any thought to how much the refinisher should earn for such *excellent workmanship?''* she demanded, her tone matching that of Mr. Masters' precisely.

"You refinished the table?" Charles said doubtfully. "You should have had it done. It wouldn't have cost much."

Eddie swung around to glare at Charles. "I finished it myself after I discovered that a professional would charge over fifteen hundred, and they weren't willing to guarantee their work. Do you know how much the very best refinishers charge by the hour? The last time I heard they were making about $50.00 an hour."

"That would still be a profit of sixty-five hundred," Charles pointed out coolly.

"Only if you used the cheapest. They rarely leave any marks behind, not even that of the original craftsman. That would have taken down the value of the table by several thousand dollars," Eddie pointed out, her voice equally cool but her eyes fiery. "Few care if the claws on the feet have toenails left when they're done. Without the toenails, you'd lose even more value."

Eddie circled the table, stopping to blow specks of dust from the surface and polish away several fingerprints with her shirttail.

"The toenails on this table had to be stripped with a tooth-pick. Did you know that?" She didn't wait for a response. "It took about ten hours. I guess having toenails costs you about five hundred dollars. For the scrolling along the edge here, I was able to use a toothbrush. The entire table took over a hundred hours. By the time you figure in the cost of my time as an *excellent workman* at fifty an hour, I don't see that there's any profit left for you."

Charles' mouth sagged open as she turned to face him squarely once again. Finally managing to close his mouth, he blustered, "But we share ownership equally."

"Of this table?" Eddie asked, her eyebrows rising. "I don't know that your name appears anywhere on the receipt for this table."

"We own this house jointly," he declared stoutly, taking a step back as Eddie advanced on him.

Hands balled into fists at her sides, Eddie took one step and then another toward Charles. She had to bite the inside of her mouth to keep from laughing when he backed away.

"That's right. We own *this house* jointly," Eddie agreed, lifting her chin a notch higher. "The contents of this house, however, are not owned jointly. They are mine. I found them. I repaired them. I own them."

"They were bought with the intention of belonging to us both," Charles argued, his voice growing louder.

"Were they?" Eddie asked, maintaining a calm voice with some difficulty. "Do you have some proof of that?"

"We were engaged," Charles shouted, forgetting his usual attitude of restraint and taking a step toward Eddie.

"Which you ..." Eddie stopped abruptly at the clatter of heels on the stairs and turned to face the new entrant into the conflict.

Chloe sailed down the stairs with more speed than Eddie had ever seen her exhibit except when her precious clothes had been threatened by the eyes of teen-age girls.

"Whatever is the problem?" she asked, joining Charles and clutching his arm.

Charles took a deep breath and patted her hand. His shoulders lifted slightly and he managed to bring an expression of bland disinterest back to his ruddy features. "Edwina and I were discussing the merits of ownership," he said in a carefully modulated tone.

"Or lack thereof," Eddie added, glowering at the clinging woman.

"There's really no reason to argue," Chloe offered, her French accent almost absent. "Charles' name is on the deed and that is indisputable."

"Agreed, but it's not on *anything* else in this house," Eddie stated. "That, too, is indisputable."

"Very well. I would have been able to almost double our

profits with the sale of your few good pieces," Charles returned, shrugging as if the money he'd expected to get from the antiques was negligible. "But if you don't want to see reason, that's your choice."

"Keeping my furniture doesn't take reason. It's just common sense. If *my few good pieces* are worth ten thousand this year, next year they might be worth twelve," Eddie retorted, the color high in her cheeks. "But it will be *my* profit, earned by the sweat of *my* brow and the work of *my* hands. You want to make a profit from antiques? Go find your own."

Chloe waved her hand dismissively in the air. "A few thousand here or there is unimportant. There will be quite enough profit from the house to compensate us all handsomely."

Eddie's eyes narrowed as the meaning behind Chloe's words dawned on her.

"There is no profit from the house," she said. "Unless you intend to sell it."

"Exactement," Chloe returned with a self-satisfied smirk.

"You'll sell this house over my dead body," Eddie fired back, releasing the anger that had been building since she'd found Charles and Mr. Masters drooling over her furniture.

"If it comes to that," Charles said, grinning at his wife who nodded her head smugly.

"You'd commit murder for a *house?*" Eddie asked incredulously, backing up a step.

"Well, not of the physical variety," Charles explained, smiling malevolently, his arm dropping from around Chloe as he began his own advance. "Perhaps professional suicide would be a more appropriate phrase."

"Professional suicide?"

"Living in sin with a man not your husband. Corrupting the morals of young people left under your charge by openly consorting with said man." Charles held his hand up and examined his manicure before glancing toward an ashen Eddie. "I believe that could be termed professional suicide, especially once the school board of Hendricksburg High is fully informed of the events.''

''How—did you—'' Eddie stammered, groping behind her for something to cling to as her knees turned to jelly. Capturing the arm of the chair before the fireplace, she dropped onto it. With trembling hands twisting together in her lap, she raised her eyes to the beaming pair above her.

''You know I've done nothing to harm my students,'' she gasped out, her voice quavery with suppressed fear.

''Perhaps, but there is a morals clause in your contract,'' Charles pointed out smugly, taking a seat on the sofa across from Eddie. ''If you'll recall, I signed a similar contract before I received word of my fellowship at the Sorbonne.''

The group before the fireplace jumped almost in unison when the front door slammed shut and Add's voice called out a greeting.

''Hi, honey. I'm home,'' he called a second time, glancing up the stairs before turning to the living room and the frozen tableau at the fireplace. His merry smile vanished the second he noted Eddie's blanched face.

''What's going on here?'' he demanded, striding across the room and dropping to his knees in front of Eddie.

''They know about us,'' she whispered through the tears that cascaded down her pale cheeks. ''Charles threatened to go to the school board.''

He pulled her into his sheltering arms and ran a rough hand over her silky head, just as he would that of a small child who'd been injured. Glaring toward the smirking pair on the sofa, he held her close as she burrowed into his hold, her tears quickly soaking his shirt.

''Gloves are off, I take it,'' he stated matter-of-factly. He noted a minuscule slippage of the smiles the other couple wore. ''So, what are your demands?''

''Edwina will agree to sign the papers for the sale of this house,'' Charles stated triumphantly. ''Any profits from such sale will be split equally.''

"How generous of you," Add retorted, his hand absently rubbing small circles up and down Eddie's back.

"We believe it's a fair and equitable arrangement," Charles replied, relaxing against the back of the sofa.

"To whom, you thieving weasel?" Add fired back coldly. "Using intimidation hardly seems fair to me."

"We could have demanded far more to insure our silence," Chloe offered, smoothing an imaginary wrinkle from her skirt before pointing out, "After all, *Ma'mselle* Mason lived rent-free in the house for the past year. She made alterations to the property that might not be acceptable to the new owner and could result in a lower selling price."

The retort in Add's throat was halted by the staccato knocking at the front door. No one moved. The knocking came again, more demanding. Sharing a questioning glance with Charles, Chloe rose and moved to answer it.

Chapter 15

"Mr. Crocker. What a surprise? Was my Charles expecting you?" she asked, placing herself between the man at the door and the three sitting silently in the living room.

"No. No. I was just in the area and wanted to get one more look at the house before I talked to some interested buyers," the man at the door replied, craning to see over Chloe's shoulder. His voice dropped. "You don't have someone interested here already, do you? You understand that if you sell the house, even without my help, the realtor's fee is still payable?"

"Of course, Mr. Crocker," Chloe assured him, repositioning herself to block his view. "We wouldn't consider excluding you from any business transaction. We were just talking to some friends."

"Good. Good," he said, his tone once again hale and hearty. He began to turn away, then suddenly turned back and raised his arm in a wave. "Hi, there. I remember you. You're the painter," he called out, eluding Chloe and barging into the living room. "I was wondering how to get in touch with you. I've got a house that needs some touch-up work before we put it on the market."

His words trailed off when Eddie lifted her tear-streaked face. She peered up at him quizzically.

"Sorry. Sorry. Didn't mean to interrupt anything," Crocker babbled, his smile slipping several notches. He thrust his hand forward. "I'm Al Crocker of Holmes Realty. We met the other day when you were doing some painting for the Whitneys." He reached into his coat pocket and pulled out a business card. "Give me a call later if you're interested."

Red-faced, he began backing away and turned to make his exit before Eddie spoke.

"I remember you. You left some papers," she said, her voice husky from crying.

"That's right," Crocker said, coming back to stand in front of her. "I dropped off some papers for you to give to Mr. Whitney regarding the sale of the house."

Eddie squirmed, jerked a crumpled paper from her pocket and began waving it wildly in the air.

"I've got it! I've got it!" she shouted, twirling around the room and finally coming to an abrupt halt in front of Charles. Waving the paper beneath his nose, she crowed, "I've got it!" before dancing away again.

Charles's face turned mottled gray as he looked first at Eddie and then at Crocker. His mouth opened and gasped for air like a dying fish.

Mr. Crocker looked at the people in the room and began backing rapidly toward the door. The smile on his face scarcely slipped when he bumped against the front door. His eyes never left the group as he called to them, "I can see this isn't a good time. I'll call later."

His hand found the knob, yanked the door open, and he escaped.

The sound of the slamming door snapped Charles out of his momentary stupor. He turned to hiss at Chloe, *"She's got it."*

Chloe's face beneath its paint and powder paled. She clutched at the back of the sofa, her nails scraping Charles's neck and drawing a yelp along with blood.

"Add, I've got it!" Eddie shouted to the ceiling before dropping into his lap and smothering his face with kisses.

Not one to fight the inevitable, Add drew her securely into his arms.

She rested her back against his chest and clutched the paper tightly in her hands. She had to blink several times before she was able to bring Charles and Chloe into sharp focus.

Eddie slowly opened the paper and began to read aloud. "Letter of commitment between Charles Biddington Whitney, Edwina H. Mason, and the Holmes Realty Company for the sale of a property located in the state of Ohio, County of Delaware. Being lot number   "

Charles turned a fulminating gaze on Chloe.

Add's smile that nearly split his face in two as the meaning of the page Eddie held became clear.

"And it's signed Charles Biddington Whitney and Edwina H. Mason," she finished triumphantly. She thrust the page toward Charles, and tapped the bottom of the paper where the two signatures were scrawled. "This is not my signature," she pointed out, jerking the paper out of reach when Chloe lunged for it.

"Now let's talk," she said, curling herself back into Add's arms.

"It . . . I . . . Chloe . . ." Charles tried but couldn't answer.

"Forgery," Add pointed out, running his fingers up Eddie's ribs until she leaned back and nipped at his ear. "Now, that's a nasty business. Perhaps you want to re-think the idea of selling this house."

Charles gulped air into his lungs, finally managing coherent speech. "Edwina wouldn't have been harmed by the sale," he defended himself. "I offered to share any profits."

Add's jaw clenched but he held his words when Eddie grasped his hand tightly and threaded her fingers intimately with his.

"Making me leave this house would have harmed me," she stated calmly, resting her hand with the incriminating paper in her lap. "Tattling to the school board about my private affairs would have harmed me. Denigrating the work I've done over the past year as nothing hurt me."

She took a deep, calming breath as her anger at her former fiance's behavior threatened to overcome her. "You're lucky I'm not a mean-spirited person like you. My demands are much more reasonable."

"Demands?" Charles asked, his voice rising an octave. A thin film of sweat began to cover his forehead.

"We will not sell this house. Nor will *we* continue to share it," she said softly, ignoring the hissed French imprecation from Chloe. "The down payment we made was eight thousand dollars. Although I believe most of that was from my salary, I'm willing to concede that it might have been fifty-fifty. That would make *your* interest in *my* house four thousand dollars."

Charles gasped, dropping his head into his hands and moaning softly.

Chloe's outraged shriek startled Add and Eddie. When she began beating Charles's shoulders with her fists and screaming French invectives, they glanced at each other and swallowed hard to hold in their laughter.

Eddie rested against Add's chest, his arms encircling her. "I think she's mad," she whispered into his ear.

"Very mad," he whispered back, teasing her earlobe with little nips.

When Chloe quieted, they turned back to the pair who now sat on opposite ends of the sofa glaring at each other. Charles' facial hue had improved somewhat, going from mottled gray to beet red.

"Are you ready to continue?" Eddie asked quietly.

Charles nodded his agreement but Chloe only stared fixedly at the fireplace.

"I'll assume all responsibility for the expenses in exchange for the deed signed over to me free and clear when I return your share of the down payment," Eddie said firmly.

"What about that paper?" Charles asked, glaring at the commitment papers and Chloe.

"As soon as you move out and the deed is signed, they're yours," Eddie returned.

"*Damnation!* Do you really think we'll just walk away? How naive you are!" Chloe rose to her feet and turned on her husband. "You fool, Charles. This house is worth seventy thousand. Do you think I'll let you walk away for a pittance? Is not *Madame* Jackson, who lives down the street, a member of the school board?"

At Eddie's gasp of outrage, Chloe seemed to grow in stature, a humorless smile lifting her lips as she nodded to Eddie. "Ah, I see I was correct. That is a problem for you, my dear. I imagine it might even be a problem for you, Mr. Rivers. I'm quite sure *Madame* Jackson will still be interested in Edwina's *vrai amour,* don't you think?" Turning back to her husband, she crowed, "You haven't lost everything, you *bouffon.* Get up and act like a man!"

Charles grabbed Chloe's arm and drew her toward him until they met nearly nose to nose.

"Don't you understand what you've done?" he demanded harshly, forcing a soft cry of pain from her as his hand tightened around her arm. "You've committed forgery. That's a criminal act. You could go to jail if she presses charges. I could be charged as an accessory. Think what that will do to *my* career. Do you think the University will keep me on? Do you think I can ever hope for advancement beyond the lowest level? That's *if* I can even get a teaching position."

Chloe gasped when he shoved her away from him and headed for the stairs. He ignored her outraged shouts for him to stop as she hurried after him. At the foot of the stairs he turned back to Eddie, cuddled comfortably on Add's lap before the fireplace.

"We'll be out of here by tonight. I'll have to arrange for someone to move our furniture at a later date," he said, staring daggers at Chloe when she came to a halt before him. With a harsh order in French he prodded her up the stairs before turning toward the living room again for a final parting shot. "Your arrangement is most irregular, Edwina. Your girls won't keep the secret forever."

Eddie and Add waited silently until they heard the door at the top of the stairs slam shut in the wake of Chloe's furious French. Eddie sighed in relief and grinned broadly up at Add.

"It's my house. All mine," she cried, pulling his head down for a soul-shattering kiss.

When they finally parted, Add lifted her from his lap and stood up beside her. His glance searched her face, noting her beaming smile, her sparkling eyes with their golden fires burning bright in triumph. Shoving his hands in his pockets, he studied the floor for a moment.

"I guess this is where I came in," he mumbled, turning away and heading for the stairs. "I'll just get my stuff packed and head back to the apartment."

His hand was on the newel post of the stairs, his foot lifted to take the first step up when Eddie's soft question reached him.

"Why?"

He threw his head back and took a deep gulp of air before he answered. "I hate to admit it but Charles is right. If I stay here, there will be questions. Both our jobs will be on the line, especially if Charles can't rein in his wife's tongue."

A loud shriek followed by a spate of enraged French punctuated his sentence.

"But I don't—"

Add looked over his shoulder. Eddie's face was crestfallen. She racked her brain for a reason to delay his departure. Tears glistened on her cheeks. His first instinct was to rush to her, comfort her, but he wouldn't allow himself the pleasure of holding her again. He'd been that route before. Unless she wanted the same things he did, there was no reason to prolong the pain for either of them.

"What don't you?" he asked, his voice harsh when he forced the words past his dry throat.

Eddie scrubbed at her tear-stained face. It seemed all she could do today was cry. Lifting her eyes, drenched with tears like morning dew on fresh grass, she met Add's questioning look.

With a cry of surrender, she ran toward him, throwing herself into his arms and burying her face in his neck.

Her tears soaked his shirt as her lilac scent drowned his senses. His arms lifted from his sides, wanting more than anything else in the world to clutch her to him. It took superhuman strength, but he resisted the urge.

They stood there like a frozen museum exhibit for long minutes while Eddie gathered the nerve to speak. Her words were muffled against his neck when she finally forced them out. "I don't want you to go. This is as much your house as mine. I want to share it with you."

Her voice faltered and he had to lay his head against hers to hear what she said next.

Her heart raced wildly in her chest.

"If it means we might lose our jobs, I don't care. I'd rather have you with me. I hate sleeping alone."

"Eddie, you love teaching, and you love the kids," Add said carefully. Afraid to push too hard, afraid not to, he waited for her to say the words he'd dreamed of her saying for nearly a year.

She slowly lifted her head. Her eyes, when they met his, sparkled with tears but there was something else there, too.

"I love you more," she managed to say, her lips lifting in a radiant smile when she said the words at last. "I love you and I don't ever want you to go away."

With a shout of joy, Add's arms surrounded her in a crushing embrace. Lifting her from the floor, he twirled her around while his lips captured hers, devouring the sweet honey taste of her, the warmth, the love that flowed freely between them.

Dizzy from their exuberant embrace, they collapsed onto the

wicker sofa. Their lips clung. Their hands explored. They reveled in the sensations that flooded them until they had to breathe or die.

"I love you, Edwina Hermione Mason." Add's raspy voice was triumphant. "I don't want to leave either. This house is special. It holds our love. I want to live here for a hundred years with you by my side."

"Well, it has survived that long," she teased, lifting her head to look around the room. "I think it can manage another hundred." Her smile slipped just a bit when she spied a sleeping bag next to the front door. "As long as we can make the payments."

"Why wouldn't we?" Add demanded, holding her above his chest so he could see her face clearly.

"Well, Mrs. Jackson," she managed before crimson flooded her face and her tongue ceased working.

"Will be happy to have Mr. and Mrs. Addison Rivers as neighbors," he finished for her. "Especially if that wild child of hers doesn't improve in math next year."

The only words that registered in Eddie's mind were *Mr.* and *Mrs.* Tears of joy began gathering in her eyes.

Add lifted Eddie's hand where his grandmother's ring hugged the third finger. "It was always meant to be there. I just wanted you to be sure." He drew her close against him after kissing her delicate fingers and the symbol of generations of love. "We'll make it official as soon as you know who leave," he promised, claiming her lips for a kiss that burned every thought from their minds.

Neither heard Charles and Chloe clatter down the stairs, banging the lovely paneling with each step. They weren't aware of the derisive snort Chloe gave when she spied them. Even the slamming of the big front door behind the departing pair went unnoticed.

Peace and tranquility settled over the house, as love held the entwined couple together. Forever.